TRUE NORTH

TRUE NORTH
SELECTED STORIES

SARA MAITLAND

ALSO BY THIS AUTHOR

Moss Witch and Other Stiories

First published in Great Britain in 2024 by Comma Press.
www.commapress.co.uk

'Moss Witch' first appeared in *When It Changed*, edited by Geoff Ryman (Comma, 2009), with consultation from Dr Jennifer Rowntree. 'A Fall from Grace' first appeared in *A Book of Spells* (Minerva, 1987). 'Andromeda' first appeared in *Telling Tales* (The Journeyman Press, 1983). 'The Beautiful Equation' first appeared in *Moss Witch* (Comma, 2014), with consultation from Prof Tara Shears. 'Miss Manning's Angelic Moment' first appeared in *A Book of Spells* (Minerva, 1987). 'Hansel and Gretel' first appeared in *Gossip from the Forest* (Granta, 2012). 'The Edwardian Tableau' first appeared in *Telling Tales* (The Journeyman Press, 1983). 'Rapunzel Revisited' first appeared in *Women Fly When Men Aren't Watching* (Virago, 1993). 'The Swans' first appeared in *Far North and Other Dark Tales* (2008). 'The Eighth Planet' first appeared in *A Book of Spells* (Minerva, 1987). 'Claudia Procula Writes a Letter' first appeared in *Angel and Me* (Mowbray, 1995). 'Why I Became a Plumber' first appeared in *On Becoming a Fairy God Mother* (Maia, 2003). 'Seeing Double' first appeared in *The New Uncanny*, edited by Sarah Eyre and Ra Page (Comma, 2008). 'Her Bonxie Boy' first appeared in *Moss Witch* (Comma, 2014), with consultation from Prof Robert Furness. 'The Pardon List' first appeared in *Protest: Stories of Resistance*, edited by Ra Page (Comma, 2017), with consultation from Prof Jane Whittle. 'True North' first appeared in *Telling Tales* (The Journeyman Press, 1983).

A CIP catalogue record of this book is available from the British Library.

ISBN-13: 978-1912697779

The publisher gratefully acknowledges the support of Arts Council England

Supported using public funding by

ARTS COUNCIL ENGLAND

Printed and bound in England by Clays Ltd.

MIX
Paper | Supporting responsible forestry
FSC® C018072
www.fsc.org

Contents

Foreword

I MET SARA MAITLAND about 35 years ago. I was trembling then on the threshold of faith, and a common friend – like her, a winner of the Somerset Maugham Award for best literary newcomer – sent me round to the vicarage where she then lived in Hackney. We talked for hours and she gave me a book, guidance and homework to help me find my way over. When I said goodbye I discovered someone had half-wrenched my bike from the railings outside. She kindly delivered what was left of it and me to the bicycle repair shop.

It was an act of supererogation, typically, and the beginning of a friendship which has shaped my life. I went straight to her writing of course, which did what her conversation did – switched on lights, opened windows, shouted, paused, hurtled from surprising angles, dazzled, dumbfounded. Talking to Sara, reading her work, makes me think sometimes of St Paul on the road to Damascus, knocked off his feet by an unexpected encounter, and the paradox of being blinded by sight.

Sara and I became neighbours in the Northamptonshire countryside and I was fortunate to see a lot of her in the year or two before she was able to embark on the solitary life she craved. You never knew what you were going to get when an invitation arrived. The company was always exciting – flamboyant clergy, academic luminaries, '60s radicals, her son's schoolfriends, the evil French archaeologist from *Raiders of the Lost Ark* – and the conversation could go anywhere. I remember massive rows about the Iraq War, penal substitutionary atonement and the Order of Precedence if the Pope and the Sovereign, with their retinues, should simultaneously arrive for dinner. Less exciting was a period, it felt long, when she worked her way through the Alice B. Toklas cookbook. I remember her once tossing a challenging salad and getting so worked up about the thirteenth century mystic Christina the Astonishing that some glossy lettuce leaves fell to the floor, where they were sniffed at by her wire-haired dachshund, Wordsworth.

Sara is someone in whose company exciting things happen. We went on trips, to Albi in southern France and she showed me the towering Doom in the pink brick cathedral there. We went to Istanbul and found Eastern Christian priests in a crypt chanting the Mass in Aramaic, Jesus's language, before being raided, mid-chant, by the Turkish police. I joined her when she spent a summer near Vicenza and on the first day broke my glasses so she spent a week interpreting for me the Palladian architecture I could not see.

Seeing again. There is a vivid, spectacular, sometimes hallucinatory quality to her speaking and her writing. It is here in her stories, charged in a way that makes me think of Gerard Manley Hopkins. Perhaps that is why her writing has such appeal for filmmakers. I remember once going to supper and she was called away to take a phone call which went on for rather a long time. 'Who was that?' I asked. 'Stanley Kubrick' (she was one of his screenwriters). Asif Kapadia is another, who turned *True North*, the title story from this collection, into the film *Far North* with Michelle Yeoh.

There is not only dazzle but discipline and high intelligence. I think you see these qualities to best effect in her short stories, so of course expert manipulators of words and images are enchanted by them. And among her circle of friends and admirers are Archbishop Rowan Williams, the best Anglican theologian of our time, and even politicians like the Clintons.

Sara now lives in the corner of Scotland where she was

born and grew up, leading a finely balanced existence of solitude with the check-ins necessary for livable life. I called in to see her last year and we talked again for hours; the papacy of Francis II, eightsome reels, the state of publishing, grandchildren. She waved me goodbye from her door and I drove towards Galloway and the setting sun, giving thanks for a wonderful friendship and a writer of such originality, challenge and excitement.

The Reverend Richard Coles,
January 2024

Moss Witch

PERHAPS THERE ARE no more Moss Witches; the times are cast against them. But you can never be certain. In that sense they are like their mosses; they vanish from sites they are known to have flourished in, they are even declared extinct – and then they are there again, there or somewhere else, small, delicate, but triumphant – alive. Moss Witches, like mosses, do not compete; they retreat.

If you do want to look for a Moss Witch, go first to www. geoview.org. Download the map that shows ancient woodland and print it off. Then find the map that shows the mean number of wet days per year. Be careful to get the right map – you do not want the average rainfall map; quantity is not frequency. A wet day is any day in which just one millimetre of rain falls; you can have a high rainfall with fewer wet days; and one millimetre a day is not a high rainfall. Print this map too, ideally on tracing paper. Lay it over the first map. The only known habitations of Moss Witches are in those places where ancient woodland is caressed by at least two hundred wet days a year. You will see at once that these are not common coordinates; there are only a few tiny pockets running down the west coasts of Scotland and Ireland. Like most other witches, Moss Witches have always inhabited very specific ecological niches. So far as we know, and there has been little contemporary research, Moss Witches prefer oak woods and particularly those where over twenty thousand years ago the great grinding glaciers pushed large chunks of rock into apparently casual heaps and small bright streams leap through the trees. It is, of course, not coincidental that these are also the conditions that suit many types of moss – but Moss Witches are more private, and perhaps more sensitive, than the mosses they are associated with. Mosses can be blatant: great swathes of sphagnum on open moors; little frolicsome tufts on old slate roofs and walls, surprising mounds flourishing on corrugated asbestos, low-lying velvet on little used tarmac roads, and weary, bullied, raked and poisoned carpets fighting for their lives on damp lawns. But Moss Witches lurk in the green shade, hide on the north side of trees and make their homes in the dark crevasses of the terminal moraine. If you hope to find a Moss Witch this is where you must go. You must go silently and slowly, waiting on chance and accident. You must pretend you are not searching and you must be patient.

But be very careful. You go at your own peril. The last known encounter with a Moss Witch was very unfortunate.

The bryologist was, in fact, a very lovely young man, although his foxy-red hair and beard might have suggested otherwise. He was lean and fit and sturdy and he delighted in his own company and in solitary wild places. Like many botanists his passion had come upon him early, in the long free rambles of an unhappy rural childhood and it never bothered him at all that his peers thought botany was a girly subject and that real men preferred hard things; rocks if you must, stars if you were clever enough and dinosaurs if you had imagination. After taking his degree, he had joined an expedition investigating epiphytes in the Peruvian rainforest for a year and had come back filled with a burning ecological fervour and a deep enthusiasm for fieldwork. He was, at this time, employed, to his considerable gratification and satisfaction, by a major European-funded academic research project trying to assess the relative damage to Western European littoral habitats of pollution and global warming. His role was mainly to survey and record Scottish ancient woodlands and to compare the biodiversity of SSSIs with less protected environments. He specialised in mosses and genuinely loved his subject.

So he came that March morning after a dawn start and a long and lovely hill walk down into a little valley, with a wide shallow river, a flat flood plain and steep sides: glacier carved. Here, hanging on the hillside, trapped between a swathe of ubiquitous Sitka spruce plantation, the haggy reedy bog of the valley floor and the open moor was a tiny triangle of ancient oak wood with a subsidiary arm of hazel scrub running north. It was a lambent morning; the mist had lifted with sunrise and now shimmered softly in the distance; out on the hill he had heard the returning curlews bubbling on the wing and had prodded freshly laid frogspawn; he had seen his first hill lambs of the year – tiny twins, certainly born that night, their tails wagging their wiry bodies as they burrowed into their mother's udders. He had seen neither human being nor habitation since he had left the pub in the village now seven miles away. He surveyed the valley from above, checked his map and came down from the open hill, skirting the gorse and then a couple of gnarled hawthorns, clambering over the memory of a stone wall, with real pleasure and anticipation. Under the still naked trees the light was green; on the floor, on the trees themselves, on rotted branches and on the randomly piled and strewn rocks – some as big as a cottage, some so small he could have lifted them – there were mosses, mosses of a prolific abundance, a lapidary brightness, a soft density such as he had never seen before.

He was warm from his walking; he was tired from his early rising; and he was enchanted by this secret place. Smiling, contented, he lay down on a flat dry rock in the sheltered sunlight and fell asleep.

The Moss Witch did not see him. His hair was the colour of winterkilled bracken; his clothes were a modest khaki green; the sunlight flickered in a light breeze. She did not see him. She came wandering along between rocks and trees and sat down very close to where he slept, crossed her legs, straightened her back and began to sing the spells of her calling, as every Moss Witch must do each day. He woke to that low strange murmur of language and music; he opened his eyes in disbelief but without shock. She was quite small and obviously very old; her face was carved with long wrinkles running up and down her forehead and cheeks; she was dressed raggedly, in a loose canvas skirt and with thick uneven woollen socks and sandals obviously made from old silage bags. Her woollen jumper was hand-knitted, and not very well. She wore green mittens, which looked somehow damp. He was still sleepy, but when he moved a little and the Moss Witch turned sharply, what she saw was a smiling foxy face and, without thinking, she smiled back.

Tinker? he wondered. Walker like himself though not so well equipped? Gipsy? Madwoman, though a long way from anywhere? He felt some concern and said a tentative 'Hello.'

Even as she did not do so, the Moss Witch knew she should not answer; she should dissolve into the wood and keep her silence. But she was lonely. It had been a very long time. Long, long ago there had been meeting and greetings and gossip among the Moss Witches, quite a jolly social life indeed with gatherings for wild Sabbats in the stone circles on the hills. There had been more wildwood and more witches then. She could not count the turnings of the world since she had last spoken to anyone and his smile was very sweet. She said 'Hello' back.

He sat up, held out his right hand and said, 'I'm Robert.'

She did not reply but offered her own, still in its mitten. It was knitted in a close textured stitch and, effortlessly, he had a clear memory of his mother's swift fingers working endlessly on shame-inducing homemade garments for himself and his sister and recalled that the pattern was called moss stitch and this made him suddenly and fiercely happy. When he shook her hand, small in his large one, he realised that she had only one finger.

There was a silence although they both went on looking at each other. Finally he said, 'Where do you come from?' Suddenly he remembered the rules in Peru about not trying to interact with people you encountered deep in the jungle. Uncontacted tribes should remain uncontacted, for their own safety, cultural and physical; they had no immunities and were always vulnerable. He shrugged off the thought, smiling again, this time at his own fantasy. There were, after all, no uncontacted tribes in Britain.

'Gondwana we think; perhaps we drifted northwards,' she said vaguely. 'No one is quite sure about before the ice times; that was the alternate generation, though not of course haploid. But here, really. I've lived here for a very long time.'

He was startled, but she looked so mild and sweet in the dappled green wood that he could not bring himself to admit that she said what he thought she said. Instead he turned his sudden movement into a stretch for his knapsack and after rummaging for a moment produced his flask. He unscrewed the top and held it out to her. 'Would you like some water?'

She stretched out her left hand and took the flask from him. Clamping it between her knees she pulled up her right sleeve and then poured a little water onto her wrist. He stared.

After a pause she said, 'Urgh. Yuck. It's horrible,' and shook her arm vigorously, then bent forward and wiped the splashes delicately from the moss where they had fallen. 'I'm sorry,' she said, 'that was rude, but there is something in it, some chemical thing and I'm rather sensitive... we all are.'

She was mad, he realised, and with it felt a great tenderness – a mad old woman miles from anywhere and in

5

need of looking after. He dreaded the slow totter back to the village, but pushed his irritation away manfully. The effort banished the last of his sleepiness and he got to his feet, pulled out his notebook and pen and began to look around him. Within moments he realised that he had never seen mosses like this; in variety, in luxuriance and somehow in joy. These were joyful mosses and in uniquely healthy condition.

There were before his immediate eyes most of the species he was expecting and several he knew instantly were on the Vulnerable or Critically Endangered lists from the Red Data Book and then some things he did not recognise. He felt a deep excitement and came back to his knapsack. She was still sitting there quite still and seemed ancient and patient. He pulled out his checklist and *taxa*.

'What are you doing?' she asked him.

'I'm seeing what's here – making a list.'

'I can tell you,' she said, 'I know them all.'

He smiled at her. 'I'm a scientist,' he said, 'I'm afraid I need their proper names.'

'Of course,' she said, 'sit down. I've got 154 species here, not counting the liverworts and the hornworts, of course. I can give you those too. I think I'm up to date although you keep changing your minds about what to call them, don't you? My names may be a bit old-fashioned.'

She chanted the long Latin names, unfaltering.

Leucobryum glaucum. Campylopus pyriformis. Mnium hornum. Atrichum undulatum. Dicranella heteromalla. Bazzania trilobata. Lepidozia cupressina. Colura calyptrifolia. Ulota crispa...

More names than he could have thought of, and some he did not even know. He sat on the rock with his list on his knee ticking them off as they rolled out of her mouth; there seemed no taxonomic order in her listing, moving from genera to genera along some different system of her own, but her tongue was elegant and nimble around the Latin names. He was both bemused and amused.

Once, he stopped her. *Orthodontium gracile* she sang, and paused smiling. He looked up and she was glancing at him quizzically. 'The slender thread moss.' She looked sly.

'No,' he said, 'no, you can't have that here. It grows in the Weald, on the sandstone scarps.'

She laughed. 'Well done,' she said, 'that was a sort of test. But I do have it. Come and see.'

She stood up and beckoned to him; he followed her round a massive granite boulder and up the slope. There behind a hazel thicket and free of the oak trees was a little and obviously artificial heap of sandstone, placed carefully in strata to replicate the scarps of Cheshire and the Weald. And there were two small cushions of *Orthodontium gracile*.

'I like it very much,' she said. 'I like it because it is a bit like me – most people don't know how to see it. It is not as rare as you think. So I invited it in.'

'You mustn't do that,' he said shocked, 'it's protected. You mustn't gather or collect it.'

'No of course not,' she said. 'I didn't. I invited it.' She smiled at him shyly and went on, 'I think perhaps you and your people are more like *Orthodontium lineare*, more successful but not native.'

Then she sat down and sang the rest of her list.

After that she took his hand in her maimed one and led him down beside the stream which gurgled and sang in small falls and cast a fine mist of spray on the banks where rare mosses and common ferns flourished. He knew then that something strange was happening to him, there in the oak wood, although he did not know what. It was magical space. It said a lot for his true devotion to bryophytes and his research that he went on looking, that he was not diverted. But time somehow shook itself and came out differently from before – and the space was filled with green, green mosses and her gentle bubbling knowledge. She spoke the language of science and turned it into a love song through her speaking and the mosses sang back the same tune in harmony.

Sometime after noon they came back to where they had started. He was hungry and got out his lunch box. She sat down beside him.

'Have you got something to eat?' he asked.

'No.'

'Do you want to share mine?'

'I'm non-vascular,' she said. 'I get what I need from the rain. That's why my wrinkles run up and down instead of across.' He looked at her face and saw that it was so. She went on, 'And of course it does mean that I revive very quickly even if I do get dried out. That's why I can go exploring, or for that matter,' she looked contented, almost smug, 'sit out in the sun with you.'

None of this seemed as strange to him as it should have seemed. He had reached a point of suspension, open to anything she told him.

'Are you...' but it did not feel right to ask her what she was. He changed the sentence, 'Are you all alone?'

'Yes, sadly,' she said in a matter-of-fact voice. 'I hoped for a long time that I would be monoicous. Nearly half of us are. But no, alas. I'm thoroughly female and as you can imagine that makes things difficult nowadays.' After a little pause she smiled at him, slightly shamefaced and said in a confessional sort of tone, 'As a matter of fact, that's what happened to my fingers. I was much younger then of course; I wouldn't try it now, but I did so want a daughter, I thought I might be clonal. You know, I'm not vascular, sensitive to pollution, often misidentified or invisible, all those things; I hoped I might be totipotent as well. So I cut off my fingers and tried to regenerate the cells. But it didn't work. It was a bad mistake. I think we must have been though, somewhere in the lineage, because of our disjunctions and wide dispersal. That's one of the problems of evolution – losses and gains, losses and gains. Vascular was a smart idea, you have to admit, even at the price of all those vulgar coloured flowers.'

He realised suddenly there were no snowdrops; no green sprouts of bluebells, wild garlic or anemone; no primrose or foxgloves. 'Don't you like flowers?'

'Bloody imperialists,' she replied crossly, 'they invaded, imposed their own infrastructure and ruined our culture, stole our land. And anyway they're garish – I do honestly prefer the elegance, the subtle beauty of seta, capsules and peristomes.'

He did too, he realised, although he had never thought of it before.

They sat together, contented, in the wildwood, in the space outside of time.

But he lacked her long patience. He could not just sit all day, and eventually he roused himself, shook off the magic, stood up and took out his collecting kit: the little glass bottles with their plastic screw tops, a sharp knife, a waterproof pencil and a squared paper chart.

'What are you doing?' she asked him.

'I'm just going to collect some samples,' he said, 'so we can get them under the microscope.'

'You can't do that.'

'Yes, it's fine,' he said reassuringly, 'I've got a certificate. This is one of the richest sites I've ever seen. We'll get a team in here, later in the year, but I need some samples now – just to prove it, you know; no one will believe me otherwise.'

'I really cannot let you do that,' she said quietly, still sitting gently on the gentle ground.

But he just smiled kindly at her and moved away up the slope. He bent over a fine little feathered mat: a *sematophyllum* – *S. micans* perhaps; he knelt down, took his knife and scraped along its underside pulling free its anchoring rhizoids and

9

removing a tiny tuft. He opened one of his bottles, popped in the small green piece and screwed up the top. So she killed him. She was sorry of course, but for witches it is always duty before pleasure.

Quite soon she knew, with great sadness, that she would have to move on. They would come looking for him and would find her, and rather obviously the crushed skull where she had hit him with the granite rock could not have been an accident.

Later still she realised that she could not just leave his body there. If they found that and did not find her, they might blame some other poor soul, some solitary inhabitant of wood or hill, some vagrant or loner. Someone like her, but not her. Justice is not really an issue that much concerns Moss Witches, but she did not want the hills tramped by heavy-footed policemen or ripped and squashed by quad bikes and 4x4s.

The evening came and with it the chill of March air. Venus hung low in the sky, following the sun down behind the hill, and the high white stars came out one by one, visible through the tree branches. She worked all through the darkness. First she dehydrated the body by stuffing all his orifices with dry sphagnum, more biodegradable than J-cloth and more native than sponge, of which, like all Moss Witches, she kept a regular supply for domestic purposes. It sucked up his body fluids, through mouth and ears and anus. She thought too its antiseptic quality might protect her mosses from his contamination after she was gone.

While he was drying out she went up the hill above the wood and found a ewe that had just given birth and milked it. She mixed the milk with yoghurt culture. She pounded carefully selected ground mosses in her pestle, breaking them down into parts as small as she could manage; she mixed the green ooze with the milk and culture.

When he was desiccated and floppy she stripped his

clothing off, rolled him onto his back among the thick mosses under the rocks and planted him, brushing the cell-rich mixture deep into the nooks and crannies of his body and pulling thicker more energetic moss clumps over his now cool flesh. At first she was efficient and businesslike, but later she allowed her imagination to cavort. She painted *Aplodon wormskioldii* on his forehead and where his toes poked up through her main planting of *Polytrichum* because it grew on the dead bodies of deer and sheep and might flourish on his bones too. She festooned his genitals with *Plagiochila atlantica* because its little curling fronds were so like the curly mass there. She carried down a rock richly coated with the lichen *Xanthoria parietina* because it was the colour of his foxy hair. She looked at her little arrangement; it was clever, witty even, and secure, but she still felt there was something missing.

After a while she knew. She went round the massive granite boulder and up the slope beyond the oak trees and behind the hazel thicket to her artificial sandstone scarp. There she hacked out one of the cushions of *Orthodontium gracile* on a piece of the reddish rock. Back where he lay she uncovered his face again, forced his mouth open and placed the sandstone in it, the little moss resting gently on his smiling lips. It was very pleasing to her, because he had been such a sweet man and knew the names of mosses.

Then she spoke clearly and firmly to all the mosses, the liverworts and the lichens she had planted. She told them to grow fast, to grow strong and to grow where she had told them. Bryophytes are not commonly obedient or compliant, they tend to follow their own rules, coming and going at their own random whim, but she knew this time they would do as she asked because they loved her. Within weeks his body would be part of the moss wood, a green irregular shape among so many others.

Then, sadly, singing all their names one last time, she

turned northwards. She climbed high up the hillside and lay down and watched the dawn. When the morning breeze came with first light, she opened her mouth wide and exhaled; and her microscopic spore flowed out between her 64 little hygroscopic teeth and was caught by the wind, and carried up into the higher air currents that circulate the Earth.

And then... well nobody knows.

Perhaps she blows there still, carried on those upper airs, waiting for a new and quieter time when witches and mosses can flourish.

Perhaps she walked north and west and came at last to another small fragment of ancient woodland, a tight ravine leading down to the sea or a small island out beyond the uttermost west, and she lives there still.

Moss Witches, like mosses, do not compete, they retreat.

Perhaps there are no more Moss Witches; the times are cast against them. But if you go into ancient woodland and it glows jewel green with moss and is damp and quiet and lovely, then be very careful.

A Fall from Grace

THOSE YEARS THE CHILDREN — in Brittany, Bordeaux and the
Loire Valley, even as far away as the Low Countries, Andalusia
and the Riviera — missed their acrobats. In the Circus, the
dingy wild animals, the clowns, illusionists and freaks remained,
but earth-bound. Gravity held the Circus, and the mud, the
stench and the poverty were more evident. The magic-makers,
the sequinned stars that flashed and poised and flew and
sparkled through the smoke above the watchers' heads, the
death-defiers who snatched the Circus from the mud and
turned it into flowers and frissons, were gone.

Gone away to the strange camp on the Champs de Mars,
where they were needed to help Monsieur E. build his
beautiful tower. Oh, the local residents might tremble in their
beds with fear at the fall from heaven; intellectuals and artists
might protest that 'Paris is defaced by this erection'. But the
Circus people, the artists of body and philosophers of balance
(with wild libidinous laughs at so unfortunate and accurate a
turn of phrase), they understood; the acrobats — without words
and with a regular fifty centimes an hour — knew. They alone
could comprehend the vision. They knew in the marrow of
their bones and the tissue of their muscles the precise tension
— that seven million threaded rods, and two and a half million
bolts could, of course, hold fifteen thousand steel girders in
perfect balance. With sinews and nerves and cartilage they did
it nightly: that tension and harmony against gravity was their
stock-in-trade. Their great delight was that Monsieur E., a
gentleman, a scientist, knew it too, and knew that they knew

and needed them to translate his vision. High above Paris they swooped and caracoled, rejoicing in the delicacy and power of that thrust, upwards, away from the pull of the ground. And so they left their Circuses, sucked towards Paris by a dream that grew real under their authority – and for two years the acrobats and trapeze artists and highwire dancers and trampolinists abandoned their musical illusions to participate in historical, scientific reality.

Eva and Louise too came to Paris. Not that they were allowed to mount up ever higher on the winches, hanging beside the cauldrons which heated the bolts white hot; not that they were permitted to balance on the great girders, shifting their weight so accurately to swing the heavy strands of lace into place. Their skill, as it happens, was not in doubt, but they were women. They drifted northwards, almost unthinkingly, with their comrades and colleagues, simply because the power of Monsieur E.'s vision was magnetic and all the acrobats were drawn inwards by it and Eva and Louise were acrobats. And they lived with the other acrobats on the Champs de Mars, poised between aspiration and reality, and the city of Paris went to their heads and they were, after a few months, no longer who they had been when they came.

Their Circus had been a disciplined nursery for such children. Born to it, they had known its rhythms, its seductions and its truths from the beginning. Precious to their parents because identical twins are good showbusiness, they were only precious inasmuch as they worked and made a show. With each lurching move of the travelling caravans, they had had to re-create the magic from the mud. Only after the hours of sweat and struggle with the tent, with the law, with the unplanned irregularities of topography, and with costumes which had become muddy or damp or creased or torn – only then were they able to ascend the snaking ladders and present the New Creation, where fear and relief were held in perfect tension; where the immutable laws of nature – gravity and pendula arches, weight, matter and velocity – were apparently defied but in fact bound, utilised, respected and controlled; where hours of dreary practice, and learning the capacities and limits of self and other, where the disciplines of technique and melodrama and precision were liberated suddenly and briefly into glamour and panache. And still were only a complete part of a delicately balanced and complete whole which included the marionette man, the clowns, the seedy lions and the audience itself.

But Paris, and a Paris in which they could not do what they were trained to do, was a holiday, a field day, where the rewards were quick and detached from the labour. As the tower grew, so did Eva and Louise, but the tower was anchored and they were free-floating. They learned to cross the laughing river and seek out the *boîtes* of Montmartre. Here, their white knickers and petticoats frothed easily in the hot water now available to them, they learned to dance the new dance – the Cancan. Here their muscularity, their training, their athleticism stood them in good stead. They were a hit: with the management who paid them to come and show off round bosoms, shapely legs, pink cheeks and bleached petticoats; with the clientele whose oohs and ahhs were more directly appreciative than those of any Circus audience.

Yes, the beauty and the energy of them as they danced and pranced and watched the tower grow and watched their comrades labour upwards. They walked under the spreading legs of the tower and laughed at the jokes called down to them; they ran among the tents and teased the labourers; they turned the odd trick here and there for affection and amusement, although they could get better paid across the river where the rich men lived, Monsieur E., coming each day to see how his dream was developing, soon learned their names and would stop and smile for them, and they smiled back, arms entwined with each other, but eyes open for everything that was going on in the world. And they reassured him of his beauty, his virility, his potency, all of which he was manifesting in his tower which broke the rules of nature by the authority of science and the power of men. One day he told them, for the simple pleasure of saying it, for he knew they were simple girls and simply would not understand, that when his tower was finished it would weigh less than the column of air that contained it. The girls laughed and wanted to know why then it would not fly away, and he laughed too, indulgently, and explained, paternally, about displacement. But from then on, the idea of the tower simply, ooh-la-la, flying away with them was fixed in Eva and Louise's minds and it made them laugh because of course they knew that it was impossible.

And walking in the streets and parks they learned new styles of dressing and new styles of living; and their eyes were wide and bright with delight. Having little to do all day they wandered here and there, through boulevards and over bridges. In the flower markets they were overcome by the banks of sweetness, the brilliance of colours; in the antique shop windows they saw the bright treasures from China and Egypt, from far away and long ago; and in the cafés they smelled new smells and heard raffish conversations about things they had not even dreamed of. And everywhere they went, because they looked so alike and smiled so merrily and were always together, people came to recognise them and smile at them, and they felt loved and powerful and free as they had never felt before. All Paris was their friend and the city itself was their Paradise.

They were a hit too in the *Salons des Femmes*, where the strange rich women, who dressed like men and caressed Eva and Louise like men too, were delighted by their health and energy and innocence. And by their professional willingness to show off. Louise enjoyed these evenings when they drank tiny glasses of jewel-coloured drinks and performed – dances, tumbles, stage acrobatics – and were petted and sent home in carriages. But Eva felt nervous and alarmed; and also drawn, excited, elated and it was not just the coloured concoctions that made her giggle all the way back to the Champs de Mars and swear that they would not go again. In the dark warmth of the bed they shared, Eva's arms would wind round Louise as they had done every night since they were conceived, but her fingers crackled with new electricity and she wondered and wanted and did not want to know what she wanted.

And of course they did go again, because it was Paris and the Spanish chestnut flowers stood out white on the streets like candles and the air was full of the scent of them, giddy, dusty, lazy. At night the city was sparkling and golden and high above it the stars prickled, silver and witty. And Monsieur E.'s tower, taut and poised was being raised up to join the two together. In the hot perfumed houses they were treated as servants, as artists and as puppy dogs, all together, and it confused them, turned their heads and enchanted them. One evening, watching them, the Contessa della Colubria said to her hostess, 'Well, Celeste, I think they won't last long, those two. They'll become tawdry and quite spoiled. But they are very charming.' 'I don't know,' Celeste said, 'they are protected. By their work of course, but not that; it must be primal innocence to love, to be one with another person from the beginning, with no desires, no consciousness.' 'Innocence? Do you think so? Perhaps it is the primal sin, to want to stay a child, to want to stay inside the first embrace, the first cell.' The Contessa's eyes glittered like her emeralds. 'Do you think it might be interesting to find out?' Celeste turned away from her slightly, watching Eva and Louise across the salon; she said quickly, 'Ah, *ma mie*, leave them be. They are altogether too young for you to bother with.' The Contessa laughed, 'But, Celeste, you know how beguiled I am by innocence. It attracts me.'

She was mysterious, the Contessa della Colubria, strange and fascinating; not beautiful *mais tres chic*, clever, witty, and fabulously wealthy. She had travelled, apparently everywhere, but now lived alone in Paris, leaving her husband in his harsh high castle in Tuscany and challenging the bourgeois gossips with her extravagance, her *outré* appearance and the musky sensation of decadence. Rumour followed her like a shadow, and like a shadow had no clear substance. It was known that she collected the new paintings, and Egyptian curios and Chinese statues; it is said that she also collected books which respectable people would not sully their homes with, that she paid fabulous sums to actresses for ritual performances, that she slid along the side of the pit of the unacceptable with a grace that was uncanny. But she had created a social space for herself in which the fear, the feeling, that she was not nice, not quite safe, became unimportant.

She took Eva and Louise home in her carriage that night. Sitting between them, her arms around each neck, her legs stretched out, her long narrow feet braced against the floor, her thin face bland, only her elongated ophidian eyes moving. The sharp jewel she wore on her right hand cut into Louise's neck, but she did not dare to say anything. The Contessa told them stories. 'You see the stars,' she said, and they were bright above the river as the carriage crossed over it. 'Long ago, long long ago, it was thought that each star was a soul, the soul of a beautiful girl, too lovely to die, too bright to be put away in the dark forever. The wild gods of those times did not think that so much beauty should be wasted, you see. Look at that star up there, that is Cassiopeia, she was a queen and so lovely that she boasted she was more beautiful than the Nerides, the sea nymphs, and they in their coral caves were so jealous and angry that they made Neptune their father punish her. But the other gods were able to rescue her and throw her up to heaven and make her safe and bright.

'And those stars there, those are Ariadne's crown; it was given to her by Bacchus who was the god of wine and passion, not an orderly god, not a good god at all, but fierce and beautiful. Ariadne loved Theseus first, who was a handsome young man, and she rescued him from a terrible monster called the Minotaur who lived in a dark maze and ate people. Ariadne gave her lover a thread so he could find his way out and a sword so he could kill the monster. But he wasn't very grateful, as men so seldom are, and he left her on an island called Naxos.'

'I know those ones,' said Louise, pointing, breaking the soft flow of the Contessa's voice with an effort, 'those ones up there, those are the Seven Sisters who preferred to be together.'

'The Pleiades, yes, how clever you are. And you see that one of them is dimmer than the others. That is Meriope, and her star is faint because she married, she married a mortal, but the rest are bright and shiny.'

Louise's neck hurt from the Contessa's sharp ring. She fell tired and uneasy. She wanted to sit with Eva, their arms around each other, tight and safe. She did not understand the Contessa. But Eva liked the stories, liked the arm of the Contessa resting warm against her skin, admired the sparkling of emeralds and eyes and was lulled, comfortable and snug, in the smooth carriage.

The balance shifted. They knew about this. As Eva leaned outwards and away, away from the centre, then Louise had to move lower, heavier, tighter, to keep the balance. As Louise pulled inward, downward, Eva had to stretch up and away to keep the balance. On the tightrope they knew this; but it was a new thing for them. There was another way, of course; their parents had had an act based on imbalance, based on difference, based on his heavy grounding and her light flying, the meeting place of the weighty and the floating. But they had not learned it. Even in the gravity-free place where they had first learned to dance together, in the months before they were born, it had been turning in balance, in precise sameness. It was the poise of symmetry that they knew about; the tension of balance. And it was foolhardy always to change an act without a safety net and with no rehearsals. They did not know how to discuss it. The difference was painful, a tightening, a loss of relaxation, of safety. The acrobat who was afraid of falling would fall. They knew that. But also the acrobat who could not believe in the fall would fall. They knew that too.

The Contessa took them to a smart patisserie on the Champs-Élysées. She bought them frothing hot chocolate, and they drank it with glee, small moustaches of creamy foam forming on their pink upper lips. They were laughing and happy. 'Which of you is the older,' she asked, 'which was born first?' 'We don't know,' said Eva and giggled. 'No one knows. We tumbled out together and the woman who was supposed to be with my mother was drunk and she got muddled up and no one knows.' 'If they did it would not matter,' said Louise. 'Our mother says we were born to the trade, we dived out with elegance.' Eva and Louise were pleased with themselves today, with the distinction of their birth, with their own inseparability, with the sweetness of the chocolate and the lightness of the little apricot tartlets. The smart folk walked by on the pavement outside, but they were inside and as pretty as any grand lady. And in the bright spring sunlight the Contessa was not strange and dangerous, she was beautiful and glamorous, she was like something from a fairy story who had come into their lives and would grant them wishes and tell them stories.

The Contessa came in her new toy, her automobile, roaring and dangerous, to seek them out on the Champs de Mars. She was driven up in her bright new chariot, and stopped right between the legs of the tower. The acrobats swarming up and down, labouring, sweating and efficient, swung aside to make space for her, as she uncoiled herself from the seat and walked among them. And she knew Monsieur E. and gave him a kiss and congratulated him on his amazing edifice. Louise did not like to see her there, but she invited them into her car and they rode off to the admiring whistles of their friends. 'In Russia,' the Contessa told them, 'the people ride in sleighs across the snow and the wolves howl at them, but it does not matter because they are snugly wrapped in great furs and the horses pull them through the dark, because it is dark all winter in Russia, and the motion of the sleigh is smooth and the furs are warm and they fall asleep while the horses run and the night is full of vast silences and strange noises so that they hang bells on the horses' bridles, and all the nobility speak in French, so that people will know how civilised they are, and not mistake them for the bearded warriors who live in snow houses beyond the northern stars. And even the women of these people wear high leather boots and ride with the men on short-legged, fierce horses. They ride so well up in that strange land that ordinary people have come to believe that they and their horses are one: they call them Centaurs, horses with human heads and trunks and arms. Long, long ago there were real Centaurs who roamed in Anatolia and knew strange things and would sometimes take little babies and train in their ways and they would grow up wise and strong and fit to be rulers, because the Centaurs taught them magic, but for ordinary people the Centaurs were very dangerous because they were neither people nor animals, but monsters.'

And they rode in the Contessa's car around the Bois and she took them back to her house and taught them how to sniff up a white powder through slender, silver straws and then they could see green-striped tigers prowling across the Contessa's garden with eyes like stars, and butterflies ten feet across with huge velvet legs that fluttered down from the trees like falling flowers. And when they went home they found they could believe that Monsieur E.'s tower could fly, and they could fly on it, away, away to a warm southern place, but they did not want to leave Paris, so they waved to the tower and they were laughed at for being drunk, and they did not tell anyone about the white powder.

One day at a party, in a new beautiful strange house where they had been invited to do a little show, the Contessa sought out Eva for one brief moment when she was alone and said, 'I have a pretty present for you.' 'Yes, madame,' 'See, it is earrings.' She held out her long, thin, dry hand, the palm flat and open, and there was a pair of earrings, two perfect little gold apples. 'These are golden apples from the garden of the Hesperides; Juno, the queen of all the Gods, gave them to Jupiter, the king of all the Gods, for a wedding present. They grow in a magical garden beyond the edge of the world and they are guarded by the four beautiful daughters of Atlas who carries the world on his back. And around the tree they grow on lies a huge, horrible dragon who never sleeps. So you see they are very precious.' Eva looked at them, amused; she had little interest in their value, but liked their prettiness. 'One for me and one for Louise, madame?' she asked. 'No, both are for you. But you will have to come by yourself one evening to my house and collect them.' 'But madame, we always go together, you know that.' 'Eva,' smiled the Contessa, 'I'll tell you a little story: once there was a woman and she was expecting a baby, and she wished and wished good things for her baby and especially that it would grow up to have good manners. Well, her pregnancy went on and on, and on and on, and still the baby was not born. And none of the wise doctors could make any sense of it. And in the end, ever more pregnant, after many, many years, as a very ancient lady, she died of old age. So the doctors, who were of course very curious, opened her up and they found two little ladies, quite more than middle-aged, sitting beside the birth door saying with perfect good manners, "After you," and, "No, no, my dear, after you". *C'est tres gentil*, but what a waste, what a waste, don't you think?' Eva giggled at the silly story, covering her mouth with her hand like a child. She did not care about the earrings but she knew that if she went to the Contessa she would find out, she would find out what it was she did not know, what it was that made her nervous and elated. She could feel too the weight of Louise, the weight of Louise inward on both of them, the weight swinging out of balance. She had to correct that inward weight with an outward one. Had to remake the balance, the inward weight with an outward one. Also she wanted to know, and if she went she would know, that and something else perhaps.

'Yes, madame,' she said, 'yes, I will come.'

And the Contessa smiled.

She did not know how to tell Louise. She could not find any words for what and why; they have never needed words before, they have not rehearsed any. Next Tuesday she would go to visit the Contessa. This week she had to find words to tell Louise. Instead, she drank. Louise, who knew she was excited but could not feel why, could not understand, could not pull Eva back to her, drank too. Their comrades on the Champs de Mars thought it was funny to see the girls drunk; they plied them with brandy and wine. Drunk, Eva and Louise showed off, they performed new tricks, leaping higher, tumbling, prancing; they do not stumble or trip, they cannot stumble or trip. They are beautiful and skilful. This is their place. The men clap for them, urging them on. In the space under the tower they dance and frolic. They start to climb, swinging upwards; from each other's hands they ascend. Somersaulting, delighting, they follow the upward thrust of the tower; its tension, its balance is theirs. The voices of the men fade below. Once, as they rise above seven hundred feet, they falter. 'It's your fault,' says Eva, 'you lean in too hard.' No,' says Louise, 'it is you, you are too far out.' But they find their rhythm again, trusting the rhythm of the tower that Monsieur E. and their hard-worked colleagues below have structured for them. On the other side of the river they can see Paris, spread out for them now, the islands in the Seine floating on the dark water, the gay streets shining with golden lights. Above, the sky is clear: the moon a bright dying fingernail, the constellations whizzing in their glory. The tower seems to sway, sensitive to their need. It is not quite finished, but as they approach the top they are higher than they have ever been, they are climbing and swinging and swooping upwards. Suddenly both together they call out to one another, 'It was my fault, I'm sorry.' The rhythm is flowing now, their wrists linked, trusting, knowing, perfect. It is their best performance ever. Down below the men still watch, although it is too dark to see. They know they will never see another show like this. They know these two are stars. They make no error. They do not fall. They fly free, suddenly, holding hands, falling stars, a moment of unity and glory.

But it is three hundred yards to the ground and afterwards no one is able to sort out which was which or how they could be separated.

Andromeda

MY MOTHER WOULD SAY that it was wrong to call one's husband a thief. Mine is. *Thief, thief, thief,* I scream at him silently.

My mother would say that it was worse than wrong to hate one's husband, to stay awake through the night and pray for his death. I do. *Die, die.* I curse him while he sleeps.

My mother would say that it was the worst crime to loathe one's children and wish they had never been born. I do that too.

My mother was a great queen, a beautiful woman and a loving mother. She fed me at her own royal breast until I was more than five years old. I can remember the sweet whiteness and warmth of her cradling me. Like a queen bee in a hive I was fed on royal jelly. I slept in her bed with her until I was nearly grown up. If I woke in the night she would stroke me and soothe me back into gentle dreams, holding me close against her own softness.

My father was a king, a true hero; he sailed with the Argonauts on the last great adventure of the golden age. I hardly knew him, but I knew his devotion to my mother and to me.

My husband is a thief, a bastard and a patricide. Perseus the Golden, son of Zeus, slayer of the Gorgon, saviour of Andromeda, founder of Mycenae. Ha.

They don't know I'm mad. No one knows I'm mad. It's my own secret. I guard it closer than I guard my life. It's mine, the only thing of my own that he has left me. I will die before I let him take that too. My madness and my hatred: fed on the milk I would not feed my children, nursed on the breast where I would not nurse my sons.

Perseus' queen walks gently through his palace, a model wife, calm but busy, her eyes lowered, veiled by her long dark lashes, an example to all young women in her modesty, her humility, the love and duty that she bears towards her husband; she seldom raises her eyes except to smile benignly at her husband's subjects or sweetly, gratefully at him.

But Andromeda is mad, mad, mad, and no one knows. In the night she roams the palace, nursing the famous dagger with which her husband killed the Gorgon, planning her thrusts, in and out, in and out; blows of vengeance that would make her more famous even than he. He claims Pallas Athena gave him her helmet to make him invisible. I need no helmet: no one is more invisible than his own good, gentle, devoted wife. That is more than helmet, it is a whole armour of invisibility, which the mad woman wears all day and is safe. Mercifully he is also a fool. There are days when I sit beside him at the table eating my meal and watching him through my meek, humble eyes, watching him shovel his food between his thick red lips, watching his coarse mouth masticate and his throat heave as he swallows it down, and wishing each mouthful was snakes' venom. And I think, *How can he be so stupid?* How can he fail to feel the waves of poison pour out of me and into his food, thrusting down and into his innards, as he has thrust his poison into mine? And then he will turn to me and say in his silly, sickly, smiling voice, 'My Andromeda, aren't you hungry? Don't you like this food? You eat like a bird, my little chicken.' And he may pick up some revolting morsel and try to feed me with his own sweaty, bloodstained hands.

When I was a child I sat on the laps of my mother's eunuchs and they would feed me sweets and peaches, their soft rounded fingers caressing my hair, and I would hop like a hummingbird from silky nest to silky nest, or come to rest against my mother's naked arm and she would reach for a grape for me; or I would bury my face in her warm sweet-smelling stomach and taste the softness of her for a dark moment.

He bangs and crashes, leaping up from the table, calling for more wine, shouting at his friends, bantering crudely, challenging someone to some absurd contest, stripping off his tunic, yelling for his horse, his slaves, his hounds, his spear. Pausing only to stroke the gold hair on his chest with a little tender gesture, he clashes outside and for hours I have to hear the wild shouts and confused arguing from the gymnasium or the arena. Then he comes puffing in again, victorious, sweaty, performing, crying out, 'Admire Me, Admire Me.' It is not an appeal, it is an expression of his conviction that I and everyone else in the world must share his admiration of himself. He believes that I admire him, because he totally believes that he is admirable. He notices nothing; no, not even the fact that his subjects and so-called friends always let him win every game, being sensible men and as aware as I am which way survival lies. Certainly he does not notice that the golden hairs he strokes are fading and yellowish, or that the famous manly chest is slipping lower. Oh yes, he's a fool my husband, as well as a thief.

But sometimes I do envy him his perfect, unshakeable arrogance and blindness. He can see everything exactly as he wants it to be. His loving wife. His fine sons, his chaste daughter. His enthusiastic subjects. And above all his heroic, wonderful self. I tell you seriously, he sincerely believes that he is actually, literally the son of Zeus. His mother's family were very strict and she was kept permanently under guard to keep her chaste. It didn't work, she became pregnant from 'a shower of gold' as popular idiom has it: the only thing that anyone knows about my husband's father is that he was rich enough to bribe the guards. But Perseus has chosen from childhood to take it literally. His mother was imprisoned, but beloved of the Gods; and Zeus disguised himself as a shower of gold in order to impregnate her. We got on rather well, his mother and I. We shared something in common; we had both been driven mad by him – she through devotion and I through hatred – mad to the point that we could see through him. We never spoke of it, but just occasionally we would exchange tiny glances of amusement, of complicity from beneath our chastely lowered lashes.

Sometimes I really cannot believe that a grown man can accept these self-created delusions as historical facts, but if you start from an unassailable assumption that you are perfect, anything and everything becomes perfectly logical. Even killing his grandfather was his destiny under heaven and NOT His Fault: nothing at all to do with his showing off and lethal competitiveness. Of course, the great advantage of being a king is that you can deal very effectively with anyone foolish enough to express a contrary opinion. Which is one of the reasons why I keep quiet. I am going to live to see him dead. With my own wifely hands I shall perform my ritual office. I am disgusted, I say publicly, by those queens who employ professional substitutes. 'How brave, how devoted, how good our queen is,' they murmur. With my own hands I am going to wipe that smug smile off his face; gently and with such joy I am going to close those pretty blue eyes; and then, when he is no longer watching me, I shall spit in his face and laugh. I shall wear the full heavy royal mourning veil when we process to his mausoleum. I shall wear it so that no one shall see the unholy glee on my face when they seal up that body for the worms to devour. Yes, yes, I long to see you then, Perseus the Golden, the favourite of the Gods, with the worms boring and thrusting down into your bloated flesh and growing fat on your decay. They are on my side, King of Mycenae. Everything you have stolen from me they will steal back again, strip away the layers of beauty and complacency, and expose what I have known from the very beginning – the stinking, putrifying foulness of your inner being, my dear husband, my own sweet royal lord. You thief, you fat, arrogant hog of a petty thief. They hang men like you daily in the courtyard and I lean out of the window, secretly, and imagine it is you, rotting, with the birds picking out your eyes. I laugh and laugh, heroic slayer of the Gorgon, to think how little those snaky tresses will help you then.

When I was a child they called me their little bird, as I pecked and chirped and sang through that sunny palace. I long and desire to chirp as I peck at your dead eyes, and to sing as the worms destroy your proud manhood.

His pride is at the root of him. He is that and nothing more. It is easy to understand. Yes, I can be understanding too, I can say how hard it must be to be a landless child, a fatherless son at the mercy of a whim of charity from foreigners, cast away unwanted and unrecognised by his own family. I can understand what that lack would do to a pretty, able child and to a passionate headstrong adolescent. I can understand how the lust to say 'Mine', to own, to possess, to lay claim to everything, would grow in a person from that background. Understand, yes. Forgive, tolerate, even care? No. No, because it is not right; but No even more because I am one of the things possessed, taken over, made into his. His. His. Everything has to be His. 'It was love at first sight,' he says of me. 'As soon as I saw her, I knew that I would run any risk, dare any adventure, if I could make her my own. Don't believe anyone who says there is no such thing as love at first sight. We knew better, don't we, my own?'

Love at first sight. It was jealousy at first sight. He was passing through Ethiopia and found that someone else was the hero of the moment. That was the intolerable thing: that someone else, not him, had laid claim to a moment of history. He could not endure that. If love was the price of grabbing one more occasion to be the Great Hero he was more than willing to pay it. But for me it was my moment. The moment that I chose, that I had dedicated to myself, my one chance, the one time when I had a choice and could offer myself as something more than the little princess, their bird, their darling. I was to be the pure, the chosen symbol of my mother's love for her people. The only acceptable sacrifice, the only freely offered gift. Can you understand? When the sea monster raged up from the deep my happy homeland was turned overnight into a place of despair. And only I could save them. I offered myself as a sacrifice for my city. The perfect sacrifice has to be offered voluntarily. I offered. What were my motives? Love, I say; my one true impulse – of love. Perhaps there were other things in it too; things that were less pure, dark poisoned things. But it was my decision for my life; my own moment of choice and I chose it. The mixture of joy and grief that greeted my offer confirmed me. They all needed me in a way that is very rarely offered to women.

How can I describe it? There was a hysteria in me and in the whole city for the week of the ritual purification. Was it here that the seeds of my madness were sown? I know that is possible, but if things had fallen out as they were meant to, what would my madness or sanity have mattered?

The rituals are complex and, to the uninitiate, uninteresting – the important fact is the growing separateness of the chosen victim. I had to move from the palace to a special, appointed room inside the temple. The day before the last day, my mother came to say goodbye to me, she was the last person allowed to do so. I had not seen my father since the second day. After this farewell, she would not be allowed to touch me or even speak to me. I lay in her arms, neither of us weeping, just tender and close. She petted me, kissed and embraced me. Her last words to me were, 'My sweetheart, I'm heartbroken, but for myself, not for you. I almost envy you. I'm glad. I love you so much, I could never have borne losing you. I always wanted to do this, to be able to keep you pure and safe and free from so much. And now you'll never have to know. Oh treasure, sweetheart. A bride of the sea, the sweet clean gentle sea. Oh my beloved, be strong.' For the last time, I buried myself in her softness, the two of us twined together, our lips against each other's. But when she went, I felt only a growing excitement and uncertainty.

In the morning, the priestesses came to dress me. The soft white dress felt like my mother's last caress, but the scent of the flowers was almost overwhelming, sweet and cloying; a heady contrast to the rich bitter smell of the incense. My head began to swim and my stomach contract in nervous, thrilling spasms. The hands of the priestesses seemed to dance over my body and my skin sang out for more. I wanted to rush into the sea, now, to have it around me, embracing me, entering and consuming me. We set off in slow procession for the half mile to the shore. The jewel-green, sheep-cropped sea grass seemed as buoyant as waves and the sea daisies too blindingly white. The sun warmed the back of my neck as it rose over the city and through the thin white robe I could feel the breeze with every corner of my skin. Where the grass comes to an end and the firm sand beach begins we stopped. About 50 yards away, where the water begins, there is a jagged outcrop of rocks on the seaward side on which I would wait, invisible from the land, totally exposed to the sea. A priestess bent down and cut my sandal thongs so that I could step out of them. I raised my arms and cried my intention to the sea, that I came freely to be given to the sea, by my people, in love and duty. Then the priestess cut the bands that held my hair, and the back of my neck was suddenly cool where it was protected from the sun. Again I called out that without ties and freely I offered myself to the sea. Then finally the priestess cut through the girdle and shoulder of my dress and it fell gently down my body. I stepped out of the pool of cloth at my feet and naked began to walk along the marked out path to the rock. Golden sand, white naked flesh, and the solemn Lament of the Maiden began. To its beautiful notes I walked round the rock and out of life.

The waves lapped my feet, cold despite the sun, and the sea was very bright. I remember quite clearly hearing the sound of the lament, feeling the cool dampness of the rock behind me and revelling in a moment of joy and fierce expectation. Then the sun seemed to quiver... a moment of unnatural stillness... four huge waves lashed out at me... beating me down... onto the rock, the hot strong waves of the monster's breath. I wanted them... fought to receive the full impact of them... embracing their thrust... feeling them soak deep into me.

I caught a glance,
hardly that,   a physical sensation
golden.   The lion that hunts
with his mane as the waves.
I don't know,
don't remember,
can't describe.
I leaned, longingly, lovingly, towards that hot mouth
to finish all things with its welcome.

And sweaty and muscle bound He ripped me from my triumph.

With the help of that serpented profanity of his, he stole my moment and made it his. I didn't know at once what had happened, but I did know, heartbreakingly, that something had gone absolutely and forever wrong. He could not allow anyone else so much as a single instant of courage or generosity. He stole it. He stole my moment, robbed me of my own choice, violated my sacrifice. He stole the one thing I had; stole it, possessed it and made it his own.

What else he and his snake friend stole from me I do not like to think of.

Well, in the eyes of the world I have been a good wife to him. I never saw that I had any choice: He stole my moment from me and I was never granted another. But my husband is a thief and, in those depths of me that even he can never ravage, I revile him.

The Beautiful Equation

IT HAD BEEN a long day and he was tired. He came into the house and was faintly relieved to realise that Derek was still at work. He went into the kitchen to make a cup of coffee. As he waited for the water to boil he noticed there was a black smear just above the power point that the kettle was plugged into. He reached out for a kitchen sponge to clean it off ('I'm getting as anal as Derek,' he thought) but just before he wiped it away he saw that it was not in any usual sense a 'smear': it was tiny writing done with a slightly smudgy felt-tipped pen. It said,

$$i\gamma^{\mu}\delta_{\mu}\Psi = m\Psi$$

He wondered a little wearily what Derek was up to now.

David McIntyre had moved back home when his mother died, and spent the next months grieving and learning with appalling clarity how much energy and love she had devoted to protecting him from his twin brother. The process was painful. It required him to rewrite the whole narrative of his life. He had come to believe, he had let himself believe, he had perhaps even encouraged himself to believe, in a way that began now to feel petulant and immature, that Derek was his mother's favourite and that he himself had never been properly loved. Worse, he had blamed her for all the difficulties he had ever encountered, emotional, professional and social. He had invented a story which exonerated him from all responsibility

– and it was founded on a fundamental self-deception. The revelation of her lifelong tactful care nearly broke his heart. In the clear space that often opens up when one dispenses with an old and clogging lie, he also knew that he had not come home in noble self-sacrifice to look after Derek as she would have wanted, but because it was a bloody nice house, nicer than anything he would be able to afford for years. He would, in exchange, have watered her beloved houseplants and cleaned her green kitchen but Derek already did those things to a densely complex, highly precise timetable that it would be insane to interfere with. So in fact all he could do was 'look after Derek'. One problem with looking after Derek was that it was nearly impossible to pin down why Derek needed looking after, though he did, or what the looking after should involve. His mother had looked after Derek. Now David learned that what that meant was loving Derek and he found that nearly impossible.

Being identical twins did not help. It was more frightening than touching to see just how very alike they were. Looking at Derek he realised just how warped one's idea of one's own face was because of seeing it only in a mirror, only flipped around, reversed. Derek looked more like him that his own mirror image did. David was two hours and nine minutes older than Derek, slightly less than an inch taller and about five pounds heavier. That was it. Since he had moved back into the house of his childhood, Derek had even taken to wearing the same clothes as David wore.

'But we won't know what's whose,' he had said with heavy patience when Derek had come home with three more shirts, identical to his favourite ones.

'Yes we will,' Derek said.

'How?'

'I can smell you on yours.' After a pause he added, 'And me on mine.'

34

And, God knows, he probably could.

Over the next few days he started to find it all over the house in unexpected places.

$$i\gamma^\mu\delta_\mu\Psi = m\Psi \quad i\gamma^\mu\delta_\mu\Psi = m\Psi \quad i\gamma^\mu\delta_\mu\Psi = m\Psi$$

He kept coming across it, bumping into it. One evening he went to look for the number of the Chinese takeaway in the Yellow Pages and discovered that Derek had written it, as neatly as ever, across the top of many of the pages; he could not decide if the pages were random or if there was some Derek type logic at work; probably the latter. But then he noticed that he too had doodled on the Yellow Pages, presumably while waiting for calls, and his doodles, though more untidy, made no more sense than Derek's.

But he did not doodle on the inside of the bathroom cabinet door; nor neatly around the tops of tins of tomatoes. Nor meticulously along the edges of the stair carpet – once for each tread; and he remembered his mother painting them years and years ago and was irritated and then irritated that he should feel irritated.

The light bulb in his bedroom failed one night and he got up crossly and went to the store cupboard to get a replacement – and found that every little box had been opened and $i\gamma^\mu\delta_\mu\Psi = m\Psi$ inscribed black on each pearl-coloured glass dome.

It became like a game of hunt-the-thimble. They had played a lot of hunt-the-thimble when they were small because Derek loved the game and was astonishingly quick. David on the other hand had been less keen; it was one of the few games in which Derek was the consistent winner – hunt-the-thimble and Pelmanism. Middle class games he had thought with contempt as a teenager and his mother allowing and encouraging them because she loved Derek best. But he caught himself looking for the $i\gamma^{\mu}\delta_{\mu}\Psi = m\Psi$ and found he experienced a childlike thrill of triumph each time he discovered a new one.

Except they began to get bigger:

$i\gamma^{\mu}\delta_{\mu}\Psi = m\Psi$
$i\gamma^{\mu}\delta_{\mu}\Psi = m\Psi$
$i\gamma^{\mu}\delta_{\mu}\Psi = m\Psi$

One day he found it written 23 times in a rigorously straight column on the back of his mother's photograph that they kept on the sitting room mantelpiece. He wondered suddenly if it had something to do with Derek grieving, the shook himself sternly: Derek did not do grief; that was one of his problems.

And anyway grief could have nothing to do with writing $i\gamma^{\mu}\delta_{\mu}\Psi = m\Psi$ in highlighter pen right across the hall mirror – to even a cunning hiding place. Except that he then had a swift passing image of his mother who never left the house without pausing to peer at herself and check that her hair was tidy.

He decided he would not mention it, he would ignore it. Perhaps he thought Derek had always written $i\gamma^{\mu}\delta_{\mu}\Psi = m\Psi$ on washable surfaces all over the house and his mother had just wiped them away. He would just wipe them away. Derek never mentioned them either. David just wiped them away.

But once, he went into Derek's bedroom. He never went into Derek's room, and Derek never came into his. They had been given separate rooms when they were about six and this privacy rule had been imposed firmly and absolutely. Now he realised that this must have been about the time that Derek had been diagnosed. And about the time his father had left. He had never put these things together before. Now he went into Derek's room with a sort of sly curiosity and some vague moral justification about 'duty of care' while knowing at some other, more honest level that it was sheer nosiness that drove him.

In size and shape, their rooms were identical. They had exactly the same decor and furniture. This he knew was no imitation or oddity of Derek's. Their mother had chosen the furniture and she had given each of them precisely the same things. He thought he had been allowed to choose his own colour schemes, changing as his growing tastes had changed, but either Derek had chosen the same or their mother had imposed it. Neither room had been redecorated since he left home. But the similarity stopped with her actions. The two of them inhabited their own space quite differently. David did not think of himself as particularly messy or slovenly, but compared to Derek he certainly was. The room was immaculate – each pen on the desk was straight; there were no clothes on the floor, nor even on the chair and Derek had made his bed before he had gone to work. Did anyone make their bed anymore? Derek did, and he had laid a white cover over the duvet with its ends tucked in, its surface unruffled. Before leaving home David had tacked adolescent posters to his blue walls and since coming back he had taken them down, leaving the darker shadows of unfaded paint behind them and he had hung three more adult paintings. Derek's walls were pristine. Except that, immediately over his bed, about a metre above his pillows, in huge black letters, was:

$$i\gamma^\mu \delta_\mu \Psi = m\Psi$$

David stood just inside the door and looked. He realised that he had no way of knowing whether Derek had written them up with obvious care and attention recently in the last few weeks or if they had been there for years.

He gritted his teeth and said nothing even when, a few days later, he found the mysterious message written on the bottom of every single plate in the cupboard. He washed them clean carefully and put them away in the tidily aligned stacks he knew Derek preferred to maintain.

And then finally he came in from jogging one Sunday

afternoon, sweaty and tired, and found

$$i\gamma^\mu\delta_\mu\Psi = m\Psi$$

gouged into the lovely pale wood of the kitchen table, each symbol at least eight inches long and irremovably deep, right across the smooth, scrubbed surface which had been the centre of his mother's life. He found himself weeping. When his twin came in he could not be silent

'Derek, what is this?'

'Call me DerAk. I've told you.'

'Oh, come on.'

'I won't talk to you if you don't call me Derak.'

'Don't be silly.' Then after a long pause, 'OK, Derak – WHAT IS THIS? Why are you writing it everywhere?'

'Because it is beautiful.'

'It is? It's not beautiful to ruin Mum's table.'

'Yes. It is so beautiful that we know it is true.'

'What.'

'Beauty is truth. Truth beauty. That is all you know on earth or need to know.'

'Derek!' There is no answer. 'OK, OK, Derak then. But what is it? Why are you doing this? I don't understand.'

'No you wouldn't.'

'Look at me.' And Derek did indeed raise his head and look straight into his brother's eyes with a benign and open gaze. But it didn't... it didn't work somehow. David knew it did not mean what it was meant to mean, what all his instincts told him it meant or should mean. Derek had done all that CBT; they had taught him to look at people when they spoke to you; to let them catch and hold your eyes; that other people liked that even if you did not, and you should do it to please them. But David knew it was an act, an empty gesture, there was nothing, no meaning in it.

He felt weary and sweaty; he wanted to take a shower and lie down. He did not want to take Derek on.

'Please Derak, please don't. Just don't scratch this... this whatever it is. Just don't do it anymore. Please.'

'OK,' said Derek, apparently completely unfazed.

'And don't draw on the walls. If you want to hang a picture up you put it on a nail. You don't write on walls. You know that.'

'OK,' said Derek again, exactly as though he had received some well-meant instructions for some activity he no particular interest in. Then his eyes drifted away, downwards, inwards and David was alone. He went up to take his shower. Derek had written $i\gamma^\mu\delta_\mu\Psi = m\Psi$ along the ceramic rim of the shower stall. David wiped it off without any thrill whatsoever and stood trying to breathe calmly under the vigorous flow of hot water.

But it seemed to have worked. David found no more graffiti over the next weeks and Derek seemed calm and busy. He felt no qualms about going off on a long-planned week's holiday with some of his friends walking in the Highlands, and annual and relaxed event. He knew his mother had happily and safely left Derek for occasional week-ends on his own once he was grown up – and he felt he had earned a break. Just as his mother had, he let a friendly neighbour know Derek was on his own in case anything complicated happened and gave her a phone number where he could be reached.

They had a wonderful five days in the harsh hills and loneliness of Wester Ross, walking high and hard during the day and drinking, eating and laughing through cheerful evenings. He did occasionally notice, internally, that the other four were now two couples, and speculate as to how he might be able to make that work for him with his responsibility for Derek. Once, he wondered if that was why his mother had never found, or even seemed to look for or want, a new partner. But it did not feel as though it mattered very much: he was content within his own body and within this old and easy companionship.

He arrived home in the early evening. As he walked down the street, the neighbour waved from her house and threw up her window. He crossed the road towards her,

'No, no,' she said, 'you get on home. Everything has been fine. He came in from work about an hour ago. He's been no trouble at all.' She smiled sweetly, shut the window and went on with her life. Something in him that he had not known was taut, relaxed. He went up his garden path with real pleasure, a sense of security and homecoming.

Every inch of every wall – in the hallway, the sitting room, and the spacious green kitchen – was covered with column after column of black symbols.

$$i\gamma^{\mu}\delta_{\mu}\Psi = m\Psi$$
$$i\gamma^{\mu}\delta_{\mu}\Psi = m\Psi$$
$$i\gamma^{\mu}\delta_{\mu}\Psi = m\Psi$$
$$i\gamma^{\mu}\delta_{\mu}\Psi = m\Psi$$
$$i\gamma^{\mu}\delta_{\mu}\Psi = m\Psi$$

There must have been over a thousand of them. And, neatly and precisely in the little space between the two lines of the equals symbol, every single equation was punctuated by a picture nail with a little bronze coloured head, hammered in with an elegant efficiency.

'Derek!'

There was no answer. He swung off his knapsack, sank onto the sofa and started to unlace his boots. All the weariness of the week leapt upon him in a single pounce, a wolf at his throat.

After a long pause he called again, 'DerAK.' Almost immediately he heard his twin come out of his bedroom and down the stairs and into the sitting room. He sat down in an armchair, looked at David and said, 'Oh, hello, it's you. Did you have a good time?'

'Yes', David said, so thrown for a moment that he had to

look at the walls again and check he had not dreamed it. He hadn't.

'Yes,' he said, 'yes, I had a very good time until just now. What the fuck have you been doing?'

'I put the nails in,' said Derek.

'I said, 'no writing on the walls'.'

'I had to,' said Derek. 'I had to. It is so beautiful and it proves me. So I know I am real.'

'What is it Derek? What does it mean? What are you talking about?'

'Look at it, stupid, look at it.'

'Don't call me stupid.'

'Well don't be stupid then. You can see, it proves me, it proves I exist. It's obvious.

'It's not obvious to me.' David suddenly heard his mother explaining to him, when he was about ten, that if you let Derek spin his story in his own way he often said interesting things. So he took a deep breath, 'Explain it to me, Derak. What is that... that maths thing you keep writing?'

'It's not a maths thing. It's a physics thing.'

'What's the difference?'

'It's for something... .if it is for something it's physics; if it isn't for something real, something that is really there, it's just mathematics. Just metaphors. I don't do metaphors, you know that.'

'OK. And what is this one for?'

'It is Paul Dirac's equation. It's a relativistic equation of motion for the wavefunction of the electron. The theory described the structure of the atom. He made it in 1932 and said that it was too beautiful to be false; that it was more important to have beauty in one's equations than to have them fit experiments.'

No one should say such bizarre things in such an uninflected monotone. David did not know how to respond.

'I see,' he said.

'No, you don't,' said Derek flatly.

'No?'

'No. Look. Look at it. You can see, I just fall out of the bottom of the equation.'

'Derek... Derak...'

'Can't you see? He predicted me. You are the electron. Everyone knows about you. I'm the positron. He predicted me and Carl Anderson found me. And they gave me to Mum.'

Then he said, 'I am your anti-particle.' After a pause he added quite casually, 'Paul Dirac had Aspergers too, you know.'

David sat and looked at the ruined walls of his mother's lovely house. He felt an infinite resigned exhaustion. But Derek was on a roll now.

'We're exactly the same, we're exactly the same but I'm different. I spin the other way. "All efforts to express the fundamental laws of Nature in mathematical form, should strive mainly for mathematical beauty. You should take simplicity into consideration in a subordinate way to beauty. It often happens that the requirements of simplicity and beauty are the same, but where they clash, the latter must take precedence." And I think it would be more beautiful if there was the same muchness of both of us. But there isn't.'

He was too tired to answer, too tired to care.

'Why isn't there, brother? Why is there more of you than of me? Why? Nobody knows why. It isn't fair. Why is there more of you than there is of me?' Derek was beginning to get het up; David knew he should soothe him, talk him down, try and engage him. He was too tired.

'Why is there more of you than of me?'

'Half an inch. And if you ate more you could be the fatter one.' He knew it was not the right answer, but he could not find the energy.

'Don't laugh at me. Don't laugh at me. Just because there

is more of you, you think you're better don't you? You think you are normal and I'm just anti, just wrong and unnecessary. But, you know what? I'm better than you. I have a positive charge. You have a negative one. That is why Mum loved me best.'

Something snapped.

After 31 years of self-control, he was the one who lost it, not Derek, not how it ought to be, not right. The weariness fell away and with it the responsibility. Furious, he hurled himself across the room, charging at Derek, like an eight-year old, a child having a tantrum, but stronger, angrier, more dangerous. And Derek rose out of the chair to meet the charge, suddenly as angry, as engaged, as involved.

Normal, thought David, *triumphant. I've made him normal.* They smashed into each other on the rug in front of the fireplace and...

... and...

'MYSTERIOUS DISAPPEARANCE OF IDENITCAL TWINS'

said the local paper the following week. It seemed to have all the right ingredients for a great story. (Our community is too small and tight-knit to want too much of a sexual angle). But from the very start it was all unsatisfactory and stuttering because there was not a single clue as to what had happened. A neighbour, who knew them well and had been an old friend of their mother's, had seen them both go into the house in the early evening. Poor Derek first: he came home from work at his usual time; his routines were very important to Derek, poor boy, he always came past at the same time. That's how she knew it was him. And dear David about an hour later. Back from some holiday, which he surely needed. What a good boy he was giving up his lovely flat and coming home to look after poor Derek when their mother died. Devoted to each other, those boys were. David had spoken to her, just briefly, just to check up on everything, as he went past. Very nicely spoken he was. Like his dear Mother. Not a day went by when she did not miss their mother; such a good friend she had been, and such a good mother. She had seen them both go into the house, definitely. No, she had not seen either of them come out. Yes, she was sure she would have noticed if one of them had – though she might well not have been able to tell us which. As alike as two halves they were.

But that did not take us very far. They had gone into the house, both of them; neither of them had come out. The house was neat and clean, no sign of any trouble. Oh yes, there were some strange drawings on the walls, quite artistic really. Someone said it had something to do with maths. Or it looked like a game they had been playing, odd but harmless. And one of them had laid out all the food and stuff for supper in the kitchen. There was not a single clue about what had happened. They had vanished.

Actually there was a clue. A small boy was walking up the road with his dog, rather late in the evening. And, suddenly he had seen strange rays of light streaming out of the house, like fireworks, but faster, brighter; straight up through the roof. And then gone. But he was not supposed to be out at that hour and had no wish to explain himself to his grown-ups so he never told anyone.

Miss Manning's Angelic Moment

WHEN SHE HAD CLOSED the shop Miss Manning decided on the spur of the moment to go to Mass. She very seldom went during the week, but this was mainly because she kept the shop open late; it made things easier for the wives who worked all day and for the men coming home who wanted cigarettes and things like that, and because she could not bear it when people said that the Asians were harder working than English people. She didn't think she was prejudiced but she also did not want it to be true, so she kept the shop open late even when her ankles felt swollen and tired. They were good friends actually, she and the family who had the nearest small shop to her; they sometimes did her cash-and-carry for her, as her nephew did for them, and they had a clear understanding about milk being for anyone but newspapers and cigarettes for her and sugar and bread for them, even when people sort of made pointed remarks. She tried to take people as she found them, she knew her duty as a Christian. On most days, she went upstairs and stayed there, or she went to the Crown, or stopped to chat to anyone who might be around. That was one of the best things about the shop: even though the town had grown and if she went to the centre, which she seldom did, she was worried about getting lost though actually she seldom did – get lost, she meant, though also she seldom went there any more. If you kept a shop people knew you and needed you and you knew them and you knew what was going on, though it way not always best to say what you knew. Her nephew said she ought to retire and that she could afford to, but she had a feeling that there would be little to do except the club and she hated gardening anyway and so she kept putting it off and putting it off, and though she knew the children laughed at her hair and nicked the sweets and that made her sad, she still liked the shop. She liked it, that was all.

So tonight she decided to go to Church. She just decided: there was no special reason but she was not the sort of woman who needed a reason for everything she did and she prepared herself to go. It was not that simple: she did not feel right going in her working overalls – though in her heart she loved the jeans the kids came in on Sundays, she did not herself want to go in her working clothes; on Sundays she always wore a hat, and not many of them did that anymore. If she put a hat on, though, people would guess where she was going and she did not fancy jokes about it the next day. But it was Church, and she had her standards and never mind what the rest of everyone thought about that. In the end she compromised with a woolly beret thing that her great-niece had given her one Christmas, a hat but definitely not a smart hat, and it was cold enough, wintry enough, for that to be unremarkable. She shut the shop, stuck a notice on the door – really she must try and organise a proper closing time and she hoped that no one would think she was ill – and ran upstairs for the beret and her prayer book, smirked at the picture of her father and thought with pleasure and guilt how he would have felt at anyone going to Church, let alone Mass, and never mind calling it Mass into the bargain, on a weekday. Then she set off for Church.

She got there rather early. Recently she had started allowing herself extra time to get to places on the grounds that she was slowing down; however, she always allowed

herself a little too much extra time so that when she arrived
too soon she could tell herself that she was not slowing down
all that much for her age. She was old enough to see through
her own little plots but they tended to make her laugh at
herself rather than be sad or angry. Only tended. She slipped
in through the west door and found the Church still in
darkness, but the light switches were all the way across the
new hall, and she could not be bothered. She knew her way
in any case to her own usual pew near the back, and she
groped her way there and settled down to her prayers. It was
strange to be in the Church in the pitch dark, and to see the
bright glowing eye of the sanctuary lamp an unmeasurable
distance away, away up by the high altar where God slumbered
not, nor slept, but she was certainly not frightened. Her papa's
children were none of them afraid of the dark, there was no
time or place for such nonsense and although she had hated
it at the time she had to admit that it did work; well, at least
for things like the dark, perhaps not for things like swimming
in the deep end, and riding the Ferris wheel – she could still
remember the sick terror grabbed in his stern arms that had
turned all fairs forever into torture chambers for her and how
hurt George had been when she would not go with him, no,
nearly 50 years ago – and all the other things that she had
never dared to do, but she did dare to be in the Church in the
dark so that was all right, and the rest better not thought of.
She had had a good life any which way. And in any case there
was nothing frightening about the Church, she had known it
all her life, driven to Sunday School and later finding there
something that the rest of her life did not somehow quite
provide, and although the dear Vicar had added a whole lot of
things when he had first come, she had got used to them all
by now, goodness what a fuss they had made back then and
here he still was and most people now saying that what he did
was what they had always done, and there was nothing to be

scared of and in a few minutes the dear Vicar would arrive and turn on the lights and light a few candles. She thought even of doing this herself, but remembered that she didn't have any matches and although she could have found the sacristy in the dark and had the key in her bag it hardly seemed worth the effort. She returned to her prayers.

Soon, indeed, the Vicar did come in and light the twin candles far away up at the Lady Altar in the side aisle. She nearly called to him that she was there, but she was right in the middle of a prayer and it did not seem right to interrupt this to chat with the Vicar so she closed her eyes and plunged on.

When, a few moments later, she looked up, she got the shock of her life. An angel was with the Vicar. The angel was, very properly, wearing a flowing white garment and was holding a branch of candles. And as she watched, the angel put the candles down on the choir stalls, went up to the Vicar, placed the angelic arms around him and kissed him, not on the forehead as she had somehow imagined that angels would kiss one, if they were to do anything of the sort, but on the mouth. The Vicar did not seem very surprised, indeed he returned the embrace and the kiss with considerable enthusiasm. Miss Manning, kneeling in the pew at the back of the Church, watched with awe. She had always known, whatever people said, that the dear Vicar was a very good, a very holy man, but even so she had not realised that he was on such very intimate terms with God's holy angels.

Then she had another shock: the angel turned away from the Vicar, so that he was facing her directly and he picked up his branched candles again. His face was thus lit up quite clearly and she saw that it was not, in fact, an angel but that young man from the polytechnic who was one of the acolytes on Sundays. Miss Manning was, genuinely, a very devout woman; she was also an old one, and in many ways thought of herself as being of the Old School, but none the less she knew a thing or two, and had not muffled herself from the world, as though anyone could who kept a corner shop in an area that she would have to admit had rather come down in the world since her day; but no, although when she had been younger she had not understood all the things that it would have been useful for her to understand, she had realised that and later had made an effort. The dear Vicar had once made a very fine sermon on just that, how it was a duty both to God and to natural intelligence to know what was going on in the real world. She had thought that this was quite right and one Lent, about six or seven years ago, she had gone so far as to make a resolution, and had read all the pages, even the business ones, of a good, quality newspaper every day – not that, in fact, it had proved such a severe penance because there had been a great many interesting things going on and she had rather come to enjoy it which had not really been the point, but only went to show when you came to think about it. However this was neither here nor there, the fact was that she knew what a homosexual was: a man who liked other men instead of women. But it was not something that she had ever really given much thought to, probably better not, although with this AIDS thing that was everywhere it was hard not to wonder a little, though the very idea that God should do that deliberately to anyone seemed to her as bad as getting the disease and she did hope that the dear Vicar... but homosexuals, she had an idea that the Bible was not in favour of it at all and that somehow it was not... not something very nice at all; in fact if she had been asked she would have said that it was wrong, and not the sort of thing that people one knew, who went to Church... and probably mostly went on in the criminal classes and other poor unfortunates whom it was one's duty to help, and anyway it was not something you had to think about very much and probably much better not to.

But this was different, the dear Vicar... that sweet young man who was such a Christian, most unusual among those young students, and so polite and kind and coming to Church nearly every day... the dear Vicar, such a good man and always visiting and not like the old Vicar in that bullying way. Well, some might not like his High Church ways – she stifled another guilty thought about her father – but everyone said how kind he was, how merry and happy... and didn't homosexuals do things in Public Toilets? Well, she would be surprised if the dear Vicar had ever been in one of those in his life, always so clean and his albs and cottas beautifully ironed and so neat always in his cassock, so much better for a clergyman than those open shirts so that one never knew where one was... but kissing that young man, whatever was his name for goodness sake? Just like a couple on their way home on Saturday nights and so brazenly, but it was not brazenly because, of course, they had not known she was there. Miss Manning realised afterwards that if it had been anywhere except the Church she might, she would have been really shocked and angry, but there, in the Church, with the candles, right up by the altar... surely the Vicar would never do anything wrong, not really wrong, not right beside the altar, not five minutes before Mass? And they had looked... well, they had looked so beautiful, she had thought it was an angel, nothing that was disgusting would make one think of an angel, would it, not ever. Of course there were Satan's wiles, but hardly public, Satan preferred craft and secrecy, she had been taught that, Satan wouldn't risk it with her in the Church and in the middle of 'Soul of Christ'. And it had been one of the most beautiful things she had ever seen, really lovely like, like... no, not like a wedding because of all the fuss that people make at weddings and that fanfare and carry-on, more like a baptism, one of those quiet little christenings that some people preferred. Of course, she knew what people would say if they knew, there were some people who would say anything, even about the dear Vicar, especially about the dear Vicar, but, she thought, and thought with pride, I don't care. She knew the Vicar was a good man, a really good man and her friend, and just kissing someone, just anything that he might do with the young student who was also a nice person, just that stuff can't make someone a bad man if they are a good person. And it had been very beautiful.

The priest and the acolyte entered and said Mass. Miss Manning said the responses to herself and when the little bell rang she did not go up for communion, she thought it would be better not to. She made a spiritual communion and was sure that that was what God would want her to do. After the service she waited, indeed it would be true to say crouched, in her pew for quite a long time and later crept out quietly and went home without passing the Vicarage, even though it made rather a long detour. She did not care. She felt decidedly happy as she ate her poached egg tea. If it made the dear Vicar happy, if he could do it right there in the Church, up by the altar, so that she thought it was an angel – though of course it was partly her own fault for being lazy about turning on the lights, and even indeed for not going more frequently to weekday Mass, despite the Vicar urging them to so often – well, if he could do it and it made him happy, which it must do because he was always so happy and not in that interfering or even frightening way that some people insisted on being happy, then it could not be a bad thing. Indeed it had to be a good thing. And also she had a secret which no one else in the whole town was going to share. Just for once in her life she was not going to be the very last person to hear something. She had her very own secret, and by keeping it she would help the Church and she would help the dear Vicar even though he would never know. She positively grinned at the picture of her father who looked down as sour and disapproving as ever.

He's dead, she told herself, and for the first time realised her own glee. Bad luck, she told the picture, you're dead and you can't make me think what you would have thought any more, you silly old man. She did not even quake inwardly. She filled herself two hot water bottles for a treat and went to bed. As she slipped between the blankets neatly, she had a delicious thought: Lent was coming up and Lent meant confession, but this time when she told the Vicar, addressing him as Father, but so different, so wonderfully different, all the private things about herself that no one else would ever know, she would know one thing about him; nothing bad, of course, she would not like that, but nonetheless a secret thing about him so that he would not be just the representative of Christ, nameless and personless behind the little grill, but real like her, only he would never know.

Hansel and Gretel

ONCE UPON A TIME there were two little children, gaunt with hunger, glazed with grief, lost in the forest. They walked hand-in-hand through tanglewood and terror until they came to a house made of gingerbread. A wicked witch lived there.

This was a long time ago. Now they are grown up; grounded and prosperous. They have never forgotten what they had learned in the woods. They used the witch's treasure trove wisely, investing first in healthy food and then in education. They continue to love and cherish each other. They always treat the world with respect and the world repays them with safety and joy.

Now Hansel is head forester to the King. He goes daily and with authority into the greenwood, walking under the trees and along small paths with knowledge and pleasure. He looks after the trees, coppice, pollard and maiden alike. He decides what can be cut and what should be cut. He interprets the Forest Laws as generously as possible, always seeking a balance between the needs of the villagers and the well-being of the trees. Some people think he lets the grazing swine back into the cut thickets a little too early, but others find his interpretation of dead wood somewhat too restrictive. He takes on young men and trains them carefully. He is well respected by his seniors and unusually popular within his community. He married a good-hearted woman, the daughter of a miller, and they have five children, and now, since this Lammastide, a first grandchild – a little girl whom they have called Gretel after his sister. He has built his house of stone, not sweet-meats; it has glass windows and stands solid against the wind and rain. It is a welcoming house of hospitality and laughter, although it is often rather untidy because he is an indulgent father. When people call him a 'warm man' it is sometimes unclear whether they mean 'rich' or 'kindly'. He is both.

With Gretel it is different. She lives alone in the forest. She is quiet, almost silent, solitary by choice. If you pass her way you will often find her in her garden. Plants – vegetables and herbs and flowers – grow well for her. Her garden is a place of colour and sweetness. She usually stands up, easing her back with her hands, and calls out a low but cheerful greeting. Once, when she was younger, she set off along the road through the forest to join the Holy Sisters in the convent at Waltham. But after a few years she came quietly home again. 'I couldn't live with enclosure,' she says calmly, if asked. Her house is built of wood with a thatched roof, but it too is sturdy and cosy. It looks rather more like a gingerbread house than Hansel's does, because it is painted in bright pale colours, and because under the eaves and around the windows are filigree strips of carved wood, which most people think are pretty but frivolous, and beside her little twisty iron gate at the bottom of her garden path there is always a bowl of sugar plums which local children know are put out for them.

The sturdy stone house and the pretty wooden house, which are neither of them like the other houses of the village, stand about two miles apart – an awkward distance: too long for a stroll, but not far enough for an expedition – so that Hansel and Gretel do not in fact meet very frequently. Sometimes if he is returning from work at Gretel's end of the forest Hansel will take a slightly longer path and pass along the hedge that runs across the bottom of her garden; and sometimes he will go in through the back gate and stand chatting while she weeds her flowerbeds, or go through her doorway and sit at her kitchen table and share a drink with her in the early evening. Or if there is a heavy fall of snow or a wild storm, Hansel will deliberately walk over to check that no harm has come to Gretel. Sometimes, though not often, some business of her own will bring Gretel to the village, and before going back under the trees she will stop by Hansel's house; he is usually out at work on these visits, but she passes neighbourly time with her sister-in-law and they like each other.

And just occasionally, for no reason that anyone can discern, often towards the end of a long summer Sunday afternoon, but sometimes at far odder hours, his wife can see that Hansel is restless. Eventually he will stand up and stretch hugely and say, as though completely by chance, 'I think I might wander over and see Gretel.' Or, 'Have you any messages for Gretel? I'm just going to pop across and see how she's doing.' And his wife will simulate a mild surprise because that is what he seems to expect and she is a good-hearted woman.

She accepts, although she does not understand, that it is like this for twins; they have a need and a sense of each other that is different from other people. She knows that his going off to visit his sister takes nothing from her and gives something to him. She knows too that, even more than other twins, Hansel and Gretel are bound together because of what happened to them when they were very young. Although she did not grow up in this village, she has heard the story. Their mother died in childbirth. Their father and his new wife tried to kill them. They ran away into... they were abandoned in... they disappeared into... they were lost in the forest. For four months no one saw hair nor hide of them. The detail is uncertain, slippery with telling. But certainly, as suddenly as they had vanished, they came home – laden with treasure and brittle with fear.

So if, just occasionally, Hansel grows restless and slips off to see Gretel in her pretty little house in the forest, his wife has no problem with that. It is so much better than the equally occasional screaming, sweating nightmares. Sometimes she will invent a message, or give him some small object to take with him; always she will send her love, and always before leaving Hansel will kiss her affectionately. And so it is today. His eldest daughter brings the baby round after Mass and they all eat together in merriment; but after the meal he feels that tug at his heart and he cannot settle. He dandles the baby, bouncing her on his knee, while she crows and grins widely. `Gretel, Gretel,' he coos to her, hoping it will dull the tug and let him stay. But eventually he gets up, gives the baby back to his daughter, smiles at his family, says that he thinks he will go over to Gretel's. He does not notice his wife shake her head minutely at his daughter, who is about to suggest coming with him. He kisses both women and goes out.

In recent years, he has marked the path to Gretel's house with white stones. It is a little joke, and he does not know if she has noticed. He watches for them one by one, and at the same time he looks at the trees which are just reaching the fullness of leaf canopy, darkening from early bright gold green to full rich green, so that less sun is finding its way through to the ground litter. Where the wood opens out into pasture ground there are wild roses, and somewhere deep in the hidden places he can hear a nuthatch chattering – zit, zit, zit – surprisingly loud for such a small bird.

Even as he walks his tension eases and he feels calmer. He suspects that Gretel no longer has this nagging need of him that he has of her – that she has somehow found her whole self inside herself and does not need him to show her who she is again. But he does not feel that this matters. He is happy as he walks through the forest in the afternoon sunshine.

The path curls round just before it breaks out of the trees and into her clearing, and for a moment he sees her – she is surrounded, covered in a cloud of white butterflies that are dancing around her face, over her shoulders and above her head. She is standing quite still, basking in their attention. He finds her briefly perfectly beautiful, and then he makes some accidental-sounding noise so that when he comes out into the clearing she has dismissed the fluttering flock and is standing there smiling at him. The chooks in their pen set up a cackle of pleasure and she calls, once, not very loudly, 'Hansel,' and he knows she is glad he has come.

He stands by her gate for a moment, and almost without thought reaches out for a sugar plum and pushes it into his mouth with an oddly greedy gesture for a grown man. She laughs and says:

Nibble Mouse, nibble mouse,
Who is nibbling at my little house?

It was what the witch had said the very first time, but now he laughs, the last of his restless tension draining away in the complete ease of her presence. He is 50 years old and munching sugar plums like a child again.

'Me,' he says, and they hug warmly.

In the kitchen she makes him drop scones, the batter waiting in a bowl beside the stove as though she had known he was coming. They eat them with the honey her bees have made. He notices she is putting on weight a little now, at last; it does not dim her loveliness for him. He watches her with pleasure as she moves graceful about her little house. They talk about little Gretel, about the hornbeam pollarding at the west end of the wood and about her strawberries and the white currants that are setting their translucent moon fruit along her wall.

Later, they go for a walk. She puts her arm round his waist and her head leans lightly on his shoulder. There is a little party of long-tailed tits, ridiculous and agitated, bustling along ahead of them; tiny pinkish balls of feathers with absurdly long tails. They do not talk much now. It is all hushed green gold and the wind has dropped away.

There is a tiny rustle, almost too small to hear, and across the path there is a ripple, a wave, a rope shaken by invisible children. It is a weasel and her two kits, in a line, crossing the path ahead of them; elegant, wicked killers with big dark eyes. The mother weasel pauses, stares at them, her white underbelly vivid on the forest floor; and then they are gone.

When Hansel looks at Gretel he sees that she is crying; silent tears run down her cheeks and she does not move to wipe them away.

'Gretel,' he says very quietly so as not to break her stillness.

'I killed her,' she says, in the same whispered tone. 'I killed our witch. I pushed her into the oven and I killed her dead. She was like a weasel, wild and fierce and free, and I killed her.'

'You had to,' he says, 'you had to. She would have killed and eaten me.'

'Would she, Hansel? Would she? I try to remember and it is all like a story. Are they true, the stories? Are they ever true?'

Sometimes they are true,' he says with great gentleness. She turns and lays her head against his chest; they stand in the sunlit wood and he holds her. 'Here is a true story. Once upon a time there was a brave little girl; she had a foolish brother, a weak and pathetic father, and an evil, cruel stepmother who certainly wanted to kill her. But in terrible fear, in the raging of danger and sadness and terror, she kept her head. She rescued them both. That is a true story.'

'And the gingerbread house? Really? And a forest that big? We know it is not that big.'

'I don't know,' he says, 'I've never known. But we were away for months and we survived. Perhaps we dreamed the witch, I don't know; perhaps we made her up so that we had some sort of story to tell. It was a dark place, a dark time and we were somewhere so bad we had to tell a story to make it bearable, to allow us to come back into the sunshine. That is what the stories are for.'

'Oh,' she says, 'thank you.' She pulls away and walks on a little and he follows her, watching her spine move as the weasels' had, flexible, graceful, lovely.

When she turns back to him she has stopped weeping, but she still looks sombre.

'You see, sometimes now I think I may be turning into our witch. I live in my little house and put out sweeties for the children. I hope they will come along the path, but when they do I sometimes feel cross or ragged with the disturbance. I wouldn't like it if they killed me and then went home and boasted about it.'

'Don't worry,' he says. 'I will not let them kill you. It is my turn to protect you now. I have grown less foolish.'

She puts her arm back round his waist and they follow the little path round towards her house.

He is shaken, because he has told the story and believed the story for years. He is shaken by her pure honesty and by her quiet lovely life. He tries to sound adult and thoughtful,

'Anyway, whatever really happened, we did learn a lot, didn't we?'

Suddenly she laughs and says, 'Well, we learned never to use breadcrumbs to make way markers with, because the birds will eat them.'

'Gretel,' he remonstrates. And then, 'OK. That was not my best moment.'

She looks slyly at him, her shadowed moment melting away now, just as his do when they are together. 'I've noticed your white stones,' she says. 'I like that.'

When they reach the gate he leaves her. He can feel that she needs to be alone now, to be silent and settled. She goes through the gate and then turns and watches as he walks across the clearing. Just when he reaches the edge of the trees she calls, 'Hansel!'

He turns and looks back at her.

'Come again soon.' She has to raise her voice so he can hear her.

'Yes,' he says, 'of course.' Then he waves and sets out for home.

An Edwardian Tableau

True to their word the Suffragists marched on the House of Commons yesterday, and the scenes witnessed exceeded in violence the utmost excesses of which even these militant women had previously been guilty.

It was an unending picture of shameful recklessness. Never before have otherwise sensible women gone so far in forgetting their womanhood.

Daily Sketch, Saturday, 19th November, 1910

DINNER SEEMED INTERMINABLE AND yet Caroline was not sure that she wanted it to end. Afterwards there were two things to be faced; she was so tired that they seemed the same, equally important, equally unimportant, it did not seem to matter. Richard would propose to her and her mother would lecture her about coming down to dinner without stays. She knew the first from her father's heartiness; Richard and he had been in the library together before the other guests had arrived; also her mother at the last, the very last moment had changed the seating so that Caroline and Richard were sitting next to each other. And would she accept him? His face moved backwards and forwards, in and out of focus, she was so tired that she did not know what she would do, what she wanted. He would be a bishop one day, they all said, he was a canon already, he was too old for her, she was too young for him, she would be a bishop's wife perhaps, perhaps not; How could she not know? How could she not care? She had known about the lecture from her mother at the very moment she had been walking down the stairs. How could she have thought that her mother, who noticed everything, would not notice? Her mother's standards, like her father's politics, were liberal but fixed, and Caroline knew every shade of them. She was allowed to smoke when there were no guests in the house; she was allowed to hunt escorted only by the groom if Graham was away, but not if he was at home and did not want to go out himself; and she could leave off stays in the daytime, but not in town and not for dinner. The lecture would cover these and other points and would include her mother's favourite little joke: 'Impropriety is one thing; indecency another.' She should not have risked it, she could not face it, the pain would have been better; no it wouldn't; even without the corset she could feel the pain, the bruise where only yesterday one of her whalebones had been snapped and driven up into her side. Hunting falls never hurt like this, but people were gentle over hunting falls and they were your own fault, or bad luck, not inflicted, deliberately, laughingly inflicted, the way Graham had hurt her when they had both been very small – run to nurse and she would make it better – but now there was no nurse and no one she could tell. She was going to fall asleep, during dinner, at the table, no, please not, please not, God. They, the They out there, her mother, her father, stout Lady Corson, the They outside her pains and tiredness were talking – listen to them, don't fall asleep, not here, not here.

They were discussing some minor corruption, some political scandal. Something mildly bad, mildly important, Caroline could not remember the details. Sir George Corson kept saying how dreadful it was, how very dreadful, how it just went to show, how monstrous it was. Caroline's mother laughed her silvery laugh – and had her laugh always been like that or had she read somewhere of a silvery laugh and set out to procure one, just as she procured good cooks and beautiful dresses? – she laughed her beautiful, silvery laugh and said, 'Of course, Sir George, these things wouldn't happen if you gave women the Vote, now that would purify politics,' because of course Caroline's mother believed in the Vote in her beautiful decorous way. Sir George responded, true to form, 'Come now Mrs Allenby, women purify the Home, you make the politicians of the future and it's far too important a job for us to let you take time off to go running in and out of polling booths. You wouldn't like it if you had to do it, and you wouldn't be in a position to purify anything then you know. No, no, women don't need the Vote, they have the sons of England to look after, and they have husbands to do the sordid things like voting for them.

'What about the unmarried women?' asked someone down the other end of the table; the conversation was going to become general, it always did when the Vote came up: there were subjects, the Vote, the Hysterical Militants, the Impossible Irish, the Ridiculous Workers, the Poor Peers, subjects that no one could resist. Sir George looked swiftly round the table, all the women were married except Caroline, who was very young, and anyway he could guess what was meant by the odd seating easily enough, so he laughed and said, 'The unmarried women? Dear Madam, there shouldn't be any, and in any case we don't want to be ruled by the failures, that's not democracy, not to my way of thinking. Remember a *Saturday Review* article that hit the nail on the head, said that a woman who failed to marry had failed in business and nothing can be done about that. I agree; may seem a little harsh at first, but think about it, think about it.' There was a little silence and then Richard raised his head and started speaking slowly, gently. Dear Richard, Caroline thought as his profile swam into focus, and yes they would make him a bishop and she would be a bishop's wife. 'It seems to me,' he was saying, 'that all this unrest is a symptom of a massive breakdown in trust. Everyone seems to be frightened, frightened and too proud. Women don't trust their men anymore and the working people don't trust us. But it does seem to me that it must in some way be our fault, and if they can't trust us then we can't be worthy of the trust and must allow them something that they do trust, the Vote, or Unions, or Home Rule or whatever it is. I think they're wrong, I think they would do better to trust people than institutions, but they don't and they must somehow be freed from their fear. There's too much fear and not enough trust and love.'

Caroline's father laughed. 'Come now, Souesby, where there are separate interests there's going to be distrust. We don't trust the workers, come to that, and I for one don't trust the Irish, neither lot of them, and I don't trust those screaming women and I don't see my way to doing so. Universal love indeed; you sound like one of those Russian Anarchist fellows.'

But Richard was not daunted; he's brave, she thought, gentle but brave, just as he was out hunting. He went on, 'That's not fair, Sir, and you won't scare me from my truth with an anarchist bogey. I'm not an anarchist, as you know perfectly well, but I will say that I've read a fair bit of their literature and I think that in there somewhere there are some pretty sound ideas. Just building up more and more institutions is not going to help any of us; we must have more trust in each other, more common interest, and stop pinning our faith on all these organisations and machines, or at least look at them more closely and see if they deserve to continue.'

Someone said, 'That's a fine way for a good churchman to talk.' He smiled and replied in his politest voice, 'Oh really, Sir, if you knew my record – a lunatic ritualist, practically an idolatrous papist, I assure you, you probably wouldn't think of me as a good churchman at all. I don't think I care so much about being a good churchman as I do about being a good man, and I still say that we all, all of us, on every side, need more love and more trust. Speaking as a churchman I could say simply that "Perfect love casteth out fear".' And even as she thought how superb he was, how her mother herself could scarcely have done it better, Caroline heard her own voice, in the distance, out there, say, 'So does hate.' And even then it might have been alright, but Richard, attentive and loving, turned round and asked quite clearly what she had said and so there was no escape. For a timeless moment her eyes seemed fixed on her mother's beautiful chest, her pure white shoulders rising up from the exquisitely ruched chiffon and the line of her neck running up past her pearls and into her lovely, lovely hair, and *why*, thought Caroline into the endless gap in time, *why don't I look like that so that I could say things like this and no one would mind?* Then she said rather loudly, 'I said, "So does hate." Perfect hate casteth out fear.' And in the astonished silence that followed she could hear her head tapping out thoughts: That will teach them, that will teach them to sit here, so pompous and liberal and benign and intelligent and talk about purity and trust and love, when outside there is anger and meanness and hate, beautiful hate which made you feel six foot tall, which made you feel as you felt when you knew that your mare was going to take in her stride a fence that others were refusing at. That will teach you Canon Richard Souesby to keep your white hands clean and turn the other cheek and trust them all while they beat you and throw you about and laugh in your face. And then Lady Corson, kind, well-meaning, fat Lady Corson said loudly and carefully, 'That reminds me of the most peculiar book I was reading, young women are so much more imaginative I think than we ever were. I wonder if you've heard of it, Mr Allenby? It's called *Dreams* by a Miss Olive Schreiner, a colonial I believe. It was lent to me by...' And they went on talking and gradually everyone joined in, but not Richard; he sat beside her, did not look at her, looked at his food, and Caroline was afraid, afraid for herself, afraid of herself, and now he would not marry her and what would she do? How would she manage without him? How could she have thought that she did not care, that it did not matter? And now he would never ask her and she loved him, she loved him, she loved him. But he did not turn round, did not smile, just sat looking at his food and eating it. And her mother's chilly white shoulders were waiting, waiting till afterwards, till all the people had gone and the fact that she was not wearing stays had ceased to matter compared to what she had done, she had silenced a whole dinner party, she had embarrassed people. The cold white shoulders and the tiredness and the dreadful, dreadful pain in her side all became one cold blur and Richard would not ask her to marry him and she was getting colder and colder and further and further away and then Emma was beside her and 'Would Miss Caroline like a glass of water?' Dear Emma, quietly pouring water and she drinking it quietly and feeling better and the room coming back towards her and she back into it, all so quietly that no one noticed. No one except Richard and he turned towards her looking concerned and asked almost soundlessly if she was alright. He smiled sweetly, lovingly, and she thought that after all he would ask her to marry him and she would accept and he would look after her always, and she felt well and strong again and started listening to the conversation.

By now it had moved on to the Awful Incident the day before, when hundreds of women had fought with the police for six hours trying to get into the House of Commons. Well, she thought, it was bound to come up, it was just bound to. She felt strong enough for it, she need not say anything, they need never know, she need only listen, even the pain seemed bearable. Sir George was talking again, 'I don't often find myself agreeing with that dreadful *Mirror*. This time I did, they hit the nail on head. *The Times* was far too soft on them. *The Mirror* said those women were a disgrace to the Empire and a source of shame to all womanhood. Couldn't agree more. Glad they left the word "ladies" out. I wouldn't even call them "women"; females, that's what they are, females. Disgusting.' And no, she couldn't keep quiet, could not listen and say nothing, could not hear her friends spoken of like that, because they were her friends, so she said, 'I was there.' She saw the ruching of her mother's dress move as her shoulders tightened, invisibly disapproving. Then one of the ladies down the table said, 'Caroline dear, I didn't know you were a militant,' and there was perhaps a hint, a slight tone of admiration, envy. It was not clear, but it was enough for Caroline to go on. 'Oh, no, I wasn't. I mean I'm not a member of the Union or anything. I was there by mistake, but I got involved, because of the crowd, and separated from Emma, there was this enormous crowd, watching them, you know.' How could she be so cool? Her mother's shoulders had relaxed again, she could go on, there would be no trouble, so long as she kept calm. 'I didn't understand the newspapers this morning, it didn't seem like that then, there, the police were very brutal.' Sir George interrupted, 'Now, now Miss Allenby, they were only doing their duty.' 'I thought,' she said, as carefully as possible, 'that it was their duty to arrest anyone who assaulted them. They wouldn't arrest us.' The shoulders tightened again. Was her whole life to be governed by the rise and fall of a pair of perfect, beautiful shoulders? 'You see,' she hurried on, 'I got involved.' Involved. There must be a better word: committed, converted. She had been standing, pushed about by the crowd, trying to see Emma, when suddenly a funny old – no not old, middle-aged – lady had fallen to the ground at her feet. She had bent down to help and asked, 'Are you all right?' But the woman was hysterical, she lay on the ground and sobbed, 'They won't arrest us, they won't arrest us, they won't arrest us' over and over again. How could she explain to these safe people how nothing had made sense, how the police were refusing to arrest them; them, us, me? 'Sir George, you don't understand, the crowd was all round, pushing in; if one tried to get out, and at first I tried very hard, I did not want to be there, I don't believe that militancy will work, I didn't see the point of it, I wanted to get out, but if you tried to leave then horrible men in the crowd pushed you back in again, back to the police and they would not arrest you whatever you did. There was an old lady there in a wheelchair, perhaps she was as mad as anything, perhaps she should have stayed at home, but she was there, and the police pulled her out of her chair and threw her to the ground and then they shoved the chair away; I saw them do that. It was very frightening, if the ladies did foolish things it was because they were frightened.' The panic had been the worst thing, she had been so frightened, so lost, so confused, turning in circles, pushing against other women, pushing them down, knocking them over herself in her desperate efforts to escape. Finally, she had run into a policeman and had grabbed him, thinking that here was safety, that he would help her, 'Get me out of here, please get me out of here.' He had seized her in his arms, crushing her so tightly that she could hardly breathe, tearing her blouse on his buttons, and he had tried to kiss her, his thick mouth on hers, and when she had protested wordlessly, determinedly, he had laughed and said, 'That's what you really want, that's what you're here for, isn't it?' She had started to struggle, kick, even bite. The policeman, suddenly angry, no longer smiling had literally thrown her onto the ground and as she landed she had felt one of her stays snap and ram itself up between her ribs. The pain and the shock had been outrageous and she had lain there with a red film running over her eyes for a moment, and then she had opened her eyes and seen the policeman standing there smiling, pointing her out to another of himself who was also smiling, but who looked almost frightened. A great wave of hatred, the sort she had not felt since she had been a little girl, filled her up, lifted her to her feet and she had realised that she was not frightened any more. She was a fighting force, she was Deborah and Joan of Arc, and Boadicea and there was no fear but only waves of beautiful hatred which make her feel six foot tall and insuperable. Hitting and shoving and insulting policemen had felt like Mafeking Night, only the bonfires were all inside her and hotter and brighter and better. But these things she could not explain, and she said, still quite calmly, to the dinner party, 'You cannot imagine how horrible it was, how frightening; some of the Members of Parliament came out on the steps to watch, they were smiling and laughing. One of them had a little child with him, she cannot have been more than ten, and he kept pointing us out to her and trying to make her laugh and she just stood there and looked amazed. He is probably a good honest man who would not go himself, let alone take his daughter to a fight, a match, whatever it is that men go to, Father, what's the word? I know, a "mill", but he still thought that seeing a thousand women abused by the police, English ladies by their own police, was a suitable amusement for her. And all those women were doing was trying to present a petition, asking for what they believe to be their rights. Apart from the Vote, surely they have a right to petition Parliament? I hated that Member of Parliament so much at that moment that, even if they had been fighting for something that I thought bad, totally wrong, I would not have left those women then, I would not have wanted to, even if I'd been able.' She was getting excited, she knew it was a mistake, that it might spoil everything, that it would do the suffrage cause no good; but her excitement was not for the Cause, it was for herself, because she had discovered that she did not need to be afraid, that she could be strong, that she need not be tied down in awe of her mother, that beauty was unimportant compared to the strength of her feelings, that militancy might not do much good for its cause but it did wonderful things for the militants. They knew what she knew, how good it was to be angry, to be really angry and show it, that when you were really angry nothing else mattered, that there was no pain, no fear, no restraint, no anything but an enormous space you could fill up with yourself and see how huge and strong you really were. She knew now how good it was to have an enemy and know that he hated and feared you, because the police had been frightened of the women and of what they had found in themselves, but that you only hated and were not frightened so that you could win, really even when they appeared to have won. And so she finished up, almost panting, 'Sir George, I have told you how dreadful it was, how humiliating and disgusting, how shameful to the Government that let it happen. I haven't told you, I cannot tell you, how fine it was, how good I felt fighting and hating the police, how good it was to abuse Members of Parliament at the top of my voice, how fine and beautiful and lovely those muddy women on the ground were, how much I loved those "Females" as you call them, when we helped each other. They have been waiting, all women. We have been waiting for 50 years for the Vote, waiting patiently to accept it as a pretty present from the men who laugh at us, who abuse us mentally and physically. I can tell you, after yesterday I am beginning to believe that after thirty years of patience and waiting and teaching calmly, Our Lord must really have enjoyed hurling over the tables of the money lenders in the temple.'

'Caroline! That is quite enough!' That was her Father, his good natured face red with embarrassment. Her mother was far calmer and far colder; 'Well, I think we've heard quite enough about the hysterical conduct of some unhappy and unbalanced women for one evening. Emma, please offer Mrs. Lettering some more of the fruit shape. Tell me Sir George, have you seen the Martins since they got back from Dresden? One can't help wondering why they've returned.'

Caroline sat at her place and the warmth she had felt died away, but she wasn't sorry, she could not be sorry, neither for what she'd done nor for what she had said. She would be sorry in the morning when she had to listen to her mother and watch the beautiful neck take on its curve of disdain; she would be sorry if Richard did not ask her to marry him and sorrier still when he married someone else, but it would not be the right kind of sorry, not the kind they would expect. That kind was out of the question now she knew how strong she could be, how it felt to be free of fear, how it felt to be totally herself. Then she looked at Richard and he was smiling, not pityingly, not even kindly, but with open admiration, even respect. For a moment she was tempted towards humility, towards wondering what she had done to deserve this wonderful man, but her courage was high and with a final triumphant rush of bravery she thought, 'Of course, I have deserved it, of course I deserve this man, of course.'

Seeing Double

HIS MOTHER HAD died when he was born. His mother had been young and at the end of a long and very hard labour, made more exhausting by the size of the baby's head. The midwife had acted promptly, gathering in the baby and carrying it away. She had washed and dressed it, before bringing it back to the mother, with a delicate lawn and lace bonnet framing its sweet little face. The mother had taken the child in her arms and smiled, though wearily; but she had made no apparent attempt to count its toes, fingers, eyes and mouths, and after a moment the midwife had turned away to her immediate duties. When she turned back the mother was dead; her face was frozen in a strange rictus, which might have been the consequence of a sudden sharp pain or might have been terror. The midwife, a woman of sturdy good sense and addicted to neither gin nor gossip, deftly massaged the mother's face back into a more seemly expression and closed her large blue eyes forever.

His father, a hero of the nation, loved, admired and honoured, but now retired to his family home in the mountains, grew gentle and sad. He spent most of his time walking in the high hills above the forest or in his library, where he was slowly but steadily compiling a taxonomy of the local flora and fauna. He took tender but perhaps slightly distanced care of his only son. He created a pleasure palace for the child – his own small suite of rooms, opening through large airy glass doorways onto a pleasant shaded portico and beyond that a delightful secluded garden with high walls, climbable trees and a pool designed for swimming in. At considerable expense, and to the irritation of the local community, he employed the midwife as a permanent nanny and found a blind but nimble servant to assist her.

The child grew, grew strong and straight and healthy. When he was old enough his father would sometimes take him up into the forests and the mountains beyond the forests where he learned the names of all the butterflies and many of the flowers. Sometimes at night they would climb together onto the roof of the house and watch the stars, and his father taught him to trace and see the patterns of the noble constellations and told him the ancient Greek stories that gave the patterns their names.

The Christmas that he was eight, his father gave him a train set and together they built and developed it. When it grew too extensive for the nursery floor, his father opened up the attics and they created a whole little world there, with electric signals and tiny model towns; and model mountains with tunnels through them, so that the boy could wait in eager anticipation for the engine to emerge from the darkness and sound its miniature horn. They made and remade ever more complicated timetables and were anxious that the trains should run on time, and not crash into each other at the points.

Each evening, after his bath, and when he was all clean and warm and ready for bed, his father would come to tuck him up and give him his good night kisses, one on each cheek and one very gentle special one on the back of his head. Then his father would pull up the hood of his pyjamas, tie the strings and say, 'God bless and keep you, little dark eyes,' and the boy would snuggle down, scarcely conscious of his own happiness.

He was twelve when he found out. One morning Nanny woke up sick – not very sick, but with a feverish headache and heavy eyes. When she did not go to the kitchen to collect the breakfast, the housekeeper foolishly sent one of the younger maids through with the tray. The boy was already up, hungry and eager, though, of course, properly concerned about nanny. He was sitting cross-legged on the sofa reading a book. The maid plonked the tray down on the little table by the window and then stood there, fidgeting. The boy did not often see people other than Daddy and Nanny and the blind servant, and he was not sure how to behave. He smiled at the girl. He had a very sweet smile, like his father's but younger and more carefree. She smiled back. She was not much older than he was and the differences between them, obvious to grown ups, were nearly invisible to them.

He said, 'Hello.'

She bobbed a sort of half-curtsey and said, 'Hello' back.

There was a pause, in which he smiled some more and she fidgeted some more.

But in the end she could not resist. For fourteen years she had heard the talk and the secret murmurs, because no respect or even love for their Squire is going to keep his tenantry from gossip about him and his, from speculation and a mild mannered sort of malice. She was curious on her own behalf, and more tempted yet by the stir she will create in the servants' hall at dinner. And he looked so sweet, with his huge dark eyes and a smile like his father's. And she might never have another chance.

'Go on,' she said, 'show us.'

He almost turned his book towards her, assuming she wanted to see the picture, but there was something, something else; even with his negligible social skills he knew there was something else.

'Show you what?' he asked, but still pleasantly, almost in

his father's kindly style, which unfortunately made her bolder.

'You know,' she said, 'it.'

The new pause was longer; he really did not know and she, better attuned, as all servants are, to the nuances of social meaning, realised that he really did not know. She had gone too far. She was embarrassed. But her shame made her even bolder.

'You know,' she said again, 'The face, the other face; the back of your head.'

Instinctively he lifted his hand to the back of his head. Through the soft flannelette of his pyjama hood, he felt the back of his head lumpy, then moving. His hand was frozen for a moment. Then he felt something bite sharply into the fleshy pad at the bottom of his thumb.

He screamed.

Suddenly Nanny was standing in the door, her hair down, grey and straggling as neither of them had ever seen it, her face flushed with her fever and fury.

'Be quiet,' she said in a commanding tone, and then losing her grip on her anger, 'Be quiet, you evil, wicked girl. Go away. Go away.'

Sobbing, the little maid ran from the room and the boy and his nanny listened to her clogs go rattling down the passage.

'Nanny?' he said, and had she been well and wakeful it might yet have been alright; she might have given him a cuddle and he would have shown her his hand and she could have magicked a pin out of his pyjama hood and told him she was a silly old nanny for leaving it there. But the headache was stronger than her wisdom and all she wanted was her bed.

'It was nothing, darling,' she said quickly, 'nothing at all. Just a silly girl. A very naughty little girl, probably trying to be funny. We won't be seeing her again. Now eat up your breakfast and go and play in the garden.'

He ate up his breakfast and went into the garden but not
to play. He had so seldom been lied to directly that he did not
understand it. Thought and speech were one in his closed
world. But he knew, he knew that nanny had made a
deliberate gap between her thoughts and her words. He went
into the garden, but not to play. There was playing, which was
not relevant; there was hearing, which was not trustworthy;
there was seeing which was not possible. There was touching
and feeling. He looked at the little red mark at the base of his
thumb, which was beginning to bruise and very tentatively,
very, very carefully, using only his fingertips and ready for
sudden attack he began to explore the back of his head.

After an hour he knew. And knowing, he knew that he
had always known. There was another face: he could feel its
nose through the flannelette of his hood, shorter perhaps than
his own, though hard to tell, but with two indentations for
nostrils, certainly; he could feel its lips though carefully with
the flat of his hand so as not to get bitten again. He knew
already it had teeth. He thought he could feel the hinge of its
jaw moving just behind his ears.

He could not untie the string of his hood, but after some
effort he worked it loose enough to pull it back from his head.
He placed his two hands delicately on the back of his head,
either side of its nose, and could feel the hollow underneath
his palms. He waited and felt a flutter, like a butterfly's footfall.
It was blinking. He pulled his hood back on and wriggled the
knot tight. He went inside and sat on the sofa again and
chanted his times tables, all the way from one-two-is-two to
twelve-twelves-are-one-hundred-and-forty-four over and
over again, all day long.

Later on, just as the day began to fade, he left his room
very quietly so as not to disturb nanny and went along the
passage to find his father. After he had passed the bottom of
the stairs that went up to the attic, he did not really know the

way. He opened various doors into various rooms all heavy with dust and cold. A huge cold dining room with twelve empty chairs and faded red velvet curtains; a room with an even bigger table covered in green cloth; there were no chairs and the edge of the table was turned up – he did not know what it was for. There was a long passage, a huge hall almost dark, and a room with little uncomfortable sofas and lots of little tables with lots of little things on them – that room was lighter, with long windows looking out over the shaggy field that his father called 'the lawn'; he had only ever seen it from high up on the hillside. That room seemed a strange thing to him because it was both beautiful and pretty. He had not known that something could be both. But his father was not there.

He came to a door with light coming out underneath it. He opened it very softly. The room was warm and clean and wonderfully untidy, with precarious piles of paper and books stacked up or lying on the floor, as nanny never let him leave his. His father was sitting with his back to the boy; his bald head inclined forward over a large desk. The boy could see that he was writing. He watched him, watched the smooth back of his skull and the slight movement of his elbow.

His father was unaware of him. After quite a long while the boy said, 'Daddy.'

His father raised his head, apparently without shock or surprise and said, 'Hello, what are you doing here? I was just going to come for you. It must have been a boring day for you with Nanny hors de combat.' He often had to guess what his father meant, and it did not worry him. 'But you must learn not to be impatient.'

'I am not impatient,' he said with dignity. 'I have come to ask you something of grave importance.'

'And what is that?' His father smiled at the formality of the announcement.

'I need to ask you why there is someone else on the back of my head.'

The boy was aware that the warm peace of the study was broken. It made him wary – his father was a hero of the nation and should not be afraid of anything. He said nothing, awkward now. After a pause his father said, 'How did you find out?' He sounded weary.

'It bit me.' The boy walked towards the desk holding out his hand.

He was almost too big to climb into his father's lap but the older man held him close, kissing the small bruise. He sagged there for a while, exhausted by the long, slow day. But it was not enough.

'But why, Daddy?'

'I don't know,' his father said, 'no one knows. It is a strange and mysterious thing.'

'Couldn't you take it away?'

'No, no, I'm afraid not. But it is not a someone, it is a part of you.' The boy could hear an odd, insistent urgency in his father's voice; and he thought it might be fear. So his father was afraid of something. The boy's world shivered, threatened. Perhaps it was his own fear that made him daring, because even as he asked, he knew it was a dangerous question. He asked, 'Is it what killed my mummy?'

'No.' But the no was too loud, too strong, too resolute. It was like Nanny's 'naughty girl'; it was true but not true; the speaker chose it to be true although there were other choices which the speaker did not choose. Grown-ups, he learned far too suddenly, spoke with double voices, cunningly, so that true and not true weren't like white and black, like either-or, like plus and minus; they were like the bogs on the hill side, shifty, invisible and dangerous.

His father's revulsion from the boy's deformity was very strong. Because he was a man of self-discipline rather than courage he would never admit this even to himself; this was why, each evening, he obliged his often reluctant lips to kiss the secret face so tenderly. This was why, too, he missed the boy's curiosity and tried to offer him consolation instead of information.

'Look,' he said, 'have I ever shown you a picture of your mother?' He turned the boy's head very gently towards a miniature set up on a filigree easel on his desk. She smiled there, all pink and blond and blue-eyed. She was pretty. But it was a picture, a painting; the boy knew that paintings did not always look like the thing they were paintings of. He could never be sure. And he did not much care; he had other things on his mind. But he understood that his father had let him into a secret place of his own and deserved some sort of thanks. He tried, slightly experimentally, to say the right thing, to do that grown-up speaking which makes a gap between the feelings and the thoughts and the words.

'I don't look much like her, do I Daddy?'

He had got it right. He felt his father smiling. 'No, you look more like me, and bad luck to you, except that men should never be that pretty.' Their dark eyes met in what the father thought was a sweet moment of male complicity and bonding. And a little later they went upstairs, hand in hand, to play with their train set.

But the day had been too difficult and his need had not been met. What he had learned was not about the other face, but about the way grown-ups did not want to talk about the other face. There was something dark and horrible about it. They were ashamed. They wanted him to keep it secret with them and from them.

But alone, alone in the darkness of night, and the deeper darkness of its invisibility, with delicate and attentive fingers, he began to explore the back of his head. He learned that what hurt it, hurt him, so he had to treat it tenderly; he learned that it blinked when he blinked, but did not smile when he smiled, or weep when he wept; he learned that its nose never dribbled, but if he pinched its nostrils closed, it did not breath through its mouth, but he became breathless; he learned that he could make it happy or angry, but that it seldom bothered to be sad.

In the end fingers were not enough. He needed to see. He could not ask.

It took him nearly two years to work it out. Then one day while the blind servant was in charge, he stole into Nanny's bedroom and borrowed the mirror from her dressing table. He took it into the bathroom and began to experiment. His father had by now taught him both some physics and how to play billiards. There had to be a way of angling the light, like angling a delicate in-off with the ivory billiard balls. If he looked in a mirror into another mirror at the right angle, he calculated that perhaps it might be possible. It was awkward. The bathroom was not designed for the purpose and its mirror was fixed to the wall.

Then, almost unexpectedly, with Nanny's mirror propped a little precariously on a tooth-mug on the windowsill, he turned his head a little and he saw what it was he was trying to see. The face was paler than his face and had no proper chin so that the mouth was angled slightly too much downwards; but he could see that its nose was very like his and its eyelashes were longer. It was prettier than he was, and it was not a painting or a picture; it was real. It opened its eyes and they were blue, as blue as the summer sky, as blue as his mother's were in her painting. Its eyes met his and it smiled, a cunning triumphant smile. It was not an it, but a She.

All women have double mouths, he thought and then he thought that he did not know where the thought had come from.

After that he could hear her voice. She whispered to

him. She used his brain to think her thoughts. She used his breath to be alive. He was never alone. And he could not tell anyone.

Sometimes it was fun – She was his friend and he had never had a friend before. They played games together, and usually he won because their feet and hands were under his management; but when he tried to run away She would come with him, following close behind, though looking in the other direction, and he could never get away.

Sometimes it was not fun – She thought thoughts he did not want to think; She said words he did not want to hear and he could never get away.

He could not have any secrets. He made his life a secret from Daddy and Nanny, but they were not real secrets because She always knew and he could never get away.

Adolescence. That was what Daddy and Nanny called it, affectionately usually, even proudly. But She called Daddy 'Papa' in a sweet little voice, which Daddy would have loved if he could have heard it; and She was mean about Nanny and refused to understand how much he needed and loved her. She complained when he wore a hat; She would wriggle and protest if he tried to lie on his back, to sleep or to look at the sky; She loved the light, and the sunshine, to which he did not like to expose her.

She hated it when he masturbated. His fingers, now well practised in delicate explorations, had new plans of their own; plans which sometimes he found appalling and sometimes found intriguing and occasionally found absolutely the most fascinating and delightful and demanding and consuming ideas in the whole wide world. She would distract him with loud noises, silly giggles, filthy words and a scathing contempt at his ineptitude, both physical and manual. He was to her both pathetic and disgusting. She was always there, and he could never get away. She had to be kept secret but he was allowed no other secrets, or privacy or silence.

When he was seventeen he fell in love. A new maid came who sang like a bird in the early morning and was soft and round with dimply cheeks, big breasts, orange hair and a merry smile. He never spoke to her, but he watched and yearned and dreamed and hoped. He wanted without knowing what he wanted. Sweet first love, or first lust without knowing the difference. But She was having none of it. She was jealous and mean and set up a shrieking in his head. Over and over again she shouted, 'Freak, freak, freak. That one will never love you – she'll only want to see me.'

When he tried shouting 'Freak' back at her like a little boy, she giggled spitefully and said, 'No, no. I don't exist. I am just the freak in you. I don't have a me. I have a you. I'm not a someone. I'm a part of you. Ask Papa.'

She said, 'That little trollop won't love you; she won't spread her legs with a Lady watching.'

'Never?' He asked her plaintively.

'Never,' She said with undisguised glee.

'I'll kill you,' he threatened.

'You can't,' she said, 'You can never get away.'

So one evening, just as the day began to fade, he left his rooms very quietly so as not to disturb Nanny and went along the passage, but not to find his father. As he passed the bottom of the stairs that went up the attic he remembered the train set with which he and his father had not played for years. It was not enough. He opened various doors into various rooms all heavy with dust and cold. Then he went downstairs to the gun room, wrote a short note for his father and shot Her through the mouth; his mouth because he couldn't get the shot gun into the back of his head.

Her Bonxie Boy

AFTER CHRISTMAS SHE went south to spend the cold months in Portugal, with her friend Alice, as usual.

In late March, she flew home. She stared out of the plane window through a gap in the clouds and imagined she could see him, beating his lonely way up the Bay of Biscay towards the Channel. But there was no urgency or even anxiety in the fantasy. She did not let herself open her laptop, but concentrated on how good it felt to know where he actually was.

One evening in the middle of February Alice had looked at her shrewdly. The fifteen years between their ages did not often bother them, but it did occasionally give Alice permission to be a little maternal.

'Has something changed?'

Helen never knew how much Alice knew, or how much she understood, if there was a difference. One reason why Alice was her friend was precisely because she was never nosy, never intruded.

'What do you mean?' she asked.

'Well usually about now you start getting edgy, start talking about leaving, going north back to your crazy island. You dither about rather fretfully. This year you seem so calm, so settled.' After a pause she added, 'I'm not trying to get rid of you, you know.' She smiled.

'Do you know something? That had not occurred to me. Isn't that nice?' They laughed and, if Alice noticed that Helen had completely ducked the question, she never gave the least sign of it.

But something had changed. And she had felt calm and settled.

It was cold and drizzling with a misty dampness when she landed, the spring seemed to be making its way north very slowly. She spent the night in her room on campus, but woke in the small hours, before the first faded light of dawn, sweating and clammy from a nightmare of big brown seabirds caught up in spinning turbines, sliced through, tossed across white-capped waves, headless, dead. She leapt out of bed and switched on her computer; the small white blip moved smoothly across the screen and she went back to sleep exhausted but reassured.

Something had changed.

In the morning she went into the department. Walking across the campus she saw two Chinese plums were in delicate pale blossom, tossing on the rough breeze, fragile but determined. There were daffodils in clumps in the grass. It all looked tidy and pretty, out of tune with her own nervous restlessness. She had a meeting with her HOD and discussed her summary of the report she had prepared while in Portugal. It was a consultation paper for the EIA of a proposed offshore wind farm. She was an internationally recognised authority on Northern European sea birds; her research centre off Lewes was well known to the small number of people who knew or cared about Northern European sea birds. This was the sort of work she undertook most winters in one form or another.

When she had been sent the original brief for this wind farm she had had a fierce moment of panic that the northern end of the proposed site would be visible from the cliffs of Allt na Croite, but she quickly realised it would not; no turbines would disrupt her long views of nothing. She then felt obliged to work particularly conscientiously to punish her inner NIMBY. But in reality she did not really know – and no one knew. It seemed realistic to suppose that periodically some birds would fly into the turbine fins and die, but it was hard to guess how many. It seemed likely that the disturbance to the sea bed would shift the patterns of fish and that introducing 108 massive structures into an environment, which had been entirely open for millions of years, might even have an effect on winds and currents, but it was difficult to calculate just what those effects might be and impossible to guess how that might impact on the birds. Differently on different species was probably the best answer.

Both she and her boss knew that there was nothing startlingly original about her meticulous report. She was using other people's research, and there was not that much. She had picked deftly at the best study, from a pair of Danish offshore wind farms in the Baltic; it was pretty solidly evidence-based. They had used both visual and radar observations and, on the whole, both travelling and feeding sea birds avoided the wind farm altogether, or flew rather elegantly between the turbines. The researchers could not and sensibly did not rule out the possibility that some birds might strike the blades which whizzed round at up to 80 miles an hour and recorded that there was a particular worry about eider ducks: they 'were concerned that these large' – she jolted in fear – 'rather clumsy' – her serenity returned – 'birds might not be able to manoeuvre around the turbines.' The Eider was not a significant species in her immediate context; but she conscientiously repeated the Danish conclusions on spacing.

She noted that lights, especially red lights, on the turbines for the sake of fishing vessels and aeroplanes might disrupt birds' electromagnetic orientation in migration and appended the current standard advice: avoid all lighting where possible, but if absolutely necessary use low-density white lights.

In the end, although she was being paid a lot of money for her thoughts, she could not really add much of significance to the RSPB's general observation:

Given the general lack of information about the specific impacts that offshore wind farms may have on birds, caution is clearly required... The available evidence suggests that appropriately positioned wind farms do not pose a significant hazard for birds... Climate change poses a much more significant threat to wildlife, and the RSPB therefore supports wind farms and other forms of renewable energy.

Her university would be pleased with her: research and impact, well paid and pleasing to the Energy Company. Honest too.

'You know, Bob,' she said, 'eventually someone is going to have to get out there in a little boat and count the birds. We could do it from Allt na Croite; it might make a nice little fourth-year project, or for one of the graduates.'

'Quite tough,' he commented. 'Can you do a risk assessment?'

'Oh blast,' she said and they both laughed. 'Perhaps we could get the Energy Company to pay for it – then we could send a local out with them.'

'Good thinking. When are you off then?' He knew her well.

'Tomorrow, I hope. Bill and Anis are supposed to come up in about four weeks and Chen Lee sometime in May. Do you need me down before that?'

'Don't think so. European Fisheries seem very happy and the grant's reconfirmed. Well done.'

In the evening she went to visit her mother. Nothing had changed. Nothing would ever change until she died. The old lady who had once been her mother smiled at her very sweetly and said that her daughter would come and visit her soon. She knew that they took extremely good care of her mother, at considerable expense which was mostly met by her brother. She knew too that the staff adored her mother and despised her for not coming more often. She no longer even tried to apologise or explain.

Later she rang her brother to tell him she was back and that she had visited their mother and found her 'well'.

'Oh,' he said, 'I should have realised you'd be back about now. I was planning on coming up this weekend myself. Why don't you hang on; it would be good to see you.'

It would be good to see him. 'Oh, I'm sorry,' she said, 'I can't. I have to get back to Allt na Croite. I'll be off in the morning.'

'I see. Your bit of rough is home from the sea, is he?' He was teasing her as he had done since she was about four years old. She did not mind.

'No,' she said, 'he's not back yet; but I'm expecting him over the weekend.'

'What exactly is it that he does? That keeps him away more than half the year?'

'I've told you. He's a sort of policeman for the Fishery people. He monitors boat catches. He's been off West Africa, in the Atlantic, this winter.'

'I still don't understand why you always have to be there first. Surely he could wait a few days.'

Even to her brother it was more or less impossible to explain; to say, 'Well, you know, he's site faithful not mate faithful. If I'm not there when he lands he'll be down the hotel with that Mhairi McLeod and I'll not see him all summer.' Instead she says, 'It's a Hebridean tradition: a woman has to be there when her man comes in from the sea. His folk would find it very strange if I wasn't. They have a hard enough time with me as it is.'

'Well, give my love to the puffins.'

'Not puffins,' she said, but laughing because he knew perfectly well it was not puffins. 'I know, I know. Everyone except research ornithologists adores puffins, so sweet and pretty – cute indeed – but actually they're a nightmare. They get in a state and then you can never know whether their behaviour is a response to your intervention or if it's real 'puffin stuff'. And, before you get onto it, not terns either, they're too flighty.'

'I know,' he says, 'when the going gets tough the terns get going. I do pay attention, you see.'

'OK, clever clogs, which sea bird am I the international expert in?'

He laughed appreciatively. 'Now you're name-dropping. But I do know: it's those big thuggish ones – with the heavy beaks and barrel-chests. They are not very bright and moderately bad tempered. But that aside they're good to research because they are quite stable.'

'Oh God, have I become that boring? You should add that skuas have commitment; they're hard working and persistent and calm, and they live a nice long time too.'

'I've just realised,' he said, 'that that has all become exactly how I imagine your boyfriend. No, little Sis, whatever you are it is never boring.'

She asked about Kate and the children.

Later he said, 'I thought I might bring your nephews up; will you still be there at half-term?'

'You've never been,' she said.

'They've been too small. I think they'd like it now. Do you remember, years ago, when we went to Muckle Flugga, and you pointed out that skua harrying the gannet; all those aerial acrobatics, that skilful ferocity. It was rather magnificent – horrible but impressive. Unfortunately I think the boys would love it.'

'Skuas drown kittiwakes too,' she said, 'just the thing for two pre-teen boys. Do come, it would be fun. It's a bit of a schlep though.'

'And I can ask your young man if his intentions are honourable.'

'They aren't,' she said. They laughed. She enjoyed him.

The next morning she left it all behind.

She stopped at the supermarket south of the Erskine Bridge for enormous quantities of coffee and then headed north up the A82, the most beautiful road in the world; the road to Allt na Croite. She drove, as always with that strange mixture of recognition, signposts and deep desire. Loch Lomondside. Crianlarich. Tyndrum. The long haunted pass through Glen Coe. Ballachulish. Fort William. Invergary.

She turns west. Her heart sings. The lovely lonely road through Kintail. Kyle of Lochalsh. The bridge, now free at last. Across An t-Eilean Sgitheanach, the winged island, with the Cuillin towering above the road, monstrous in their ferocity. Portree. Uig, where the road ends at the bottom of the steep curling hill. She is going beyond. Outwith the harbour wall there is nothing but sea and work and love and joy.

She is tired now. She has to wait for the ferry. It is cold and beyond the harbour wall the Minch is quite rough. She buys a beer in the bar and drinks it on her own. The ferry is not very full.

From Tarbert she sets off in a caterpillar of cars along the narrow road, but gradually the drivers peel off; she is alone, her headlights picking out the lochans as sheets of dark metal along the roadsides. The sea is close. She can feel it even when she cannot see it or hear it above the car engine. In the village she parks the car and goes into the hotel.

She is welcome. Although she has not told anyone she is coming, she knows they are pleased. Even Mhairi McLeod, who goes behind the reception desk and finds a bedroom key.

'Come down when you're ready,' she says, 'Iain's in the bar tonight.'

She sits on the bed and opens her laptop. All day she has not looked and now she does. He is above the top of Ireland, though farther west, standing well out to sea and moving northwards steadily. He might arrive tomorrow. She smiles.

In the bar the men greet her with pleasure. 'Helen! Do bheatha dhan dùthaich! Ciamar a tha?'

She fumbles the response. She can just about say, 'Shin sibh. 'S math bhith air ais,' and they laugh at her accent. Someone orders her a drink.

'Bha sinn an dùil nach b' fhada gus am biodh tu air ais,' one of the old men said and then said it again in English, 'We were saying so. The bonxies are coming in now. Saw a first one four days back.'

They exchange news from the winter. It is her eleventh year... They know who she is; without belonging, which she knows she never will, she is accepted. They may even be proud of her; certainly there are pictures from the *Colour Supplement* article about her research centre on the wall of the bar. They speak in English for her.

'So, Iain,' she says later, 'any winter damage?'

'No, Dougie and I went over ten days ago to have a look. Everything's fine.'

'Can you take me out tomorrow?'

Suddenly the bar is silent. Iain lowers his eyes to inspect his glass. The old men tut audibly; two of the younger men catch each other's eye, grinning perhaps nervously.

'Helen.' Iain sounds reproving. She is startled. There is a pause.

'Helen, what day is it today?'

'Saturday.' She is confused, almost interrogative.

'So, what day is it tomorrow?'

'Sund... Oh Iain, I'm sorry, I forgot.'

'Well, don't.' Then he smiles, laughing at her, momentarily like her brother. 'It's lucky you've come back from the godless lands. We can put you right.'

The Sabbatarianism still seems weird to her. But she should not have forgotten. She hears a small echo of the anxious fret that has driven her thousands of miles north in just three days. So near and yet so far; she needs to get out there. He is clear of Ireland now, out there somewhere in the dark. But she will not argue this one. She accepts her guest status. She likes it in fact.

Later she prepares to go upstairs.

'First thing Monday,' Iain says. 'I'll come and help you load up − we'll want to be away before nine. For the tide. I'll see you in the harbour.'

'I'll be at Kirk tomorrow,' she says.

'Guilt? You don't have to.'

'No, for the singing.'

'Tell you a funny thing,' Iain says. 'Last autumn we had an invasion. It was three Baptist ministers, and two of their wives, from Alabama. You can imagine. Half the children have never seen a non-white person... Well apparently, down in the Southern states, they sing like we do − they call it 'lining' but it's just the same as Gaelic psalms. The precentor gives the line and the congregation pick it up. Different tunes, but the same thing, unaccompanied − but we're meant to say a cappella we learned. Theirs is a bit more cheerful and for me a bit less haunting, but it is the same. And − well, they'd come because some American professor of music has been saying that the Southern Baptists got their singing, their 'lining', from here, from the Islands. Well, they did not want that to be true, because they've always thought it came from Africa and was their heritage from before slavery, and we didn't want it to be true because you know us − we don't really care for the idea that folk went from here and got rich and kept slaves − not our self-image, not Free Kirk. So here's both lots not wanting it. But one of them has the real God craic so the minister is all keen on him, and we end up singing for each other in the

Kirk like a Céilídh. Then it turns out one of their women gives the line and the minister doesn't like that so much. But, I think we all knew the professor chap, who is neither black nor Scottish, was right... The music migrating all that way. It made me think of you and your birds.'

It is a long speech for him. They smile at each other. And on Sunday, in the morning, she goes to the Kirk and hears that beautiful tragic singing and in the afternoon walks round the Calanais standing stones in the magical peace of the island Sabbath and feels soothed, briefly at rest.

It does not last. She wakes too early on Monday morning, before it is light and she cannot get a broadband connection and is fretful. The coffee is nasty and she does not want porridge; she wants to be going. He might have come last night.

She reverses her car down onto the quay, and starts unloading the boxes from the back. There are very few boats riding on the still water inside the grey rampart at this time of year, but there are two female Eider ducks bobbing close in among the seaweed patches. The light increases; the wind, even in the harbour, is fresh; the grey of the sky breaks into elegant long bands of cloud. Although she feels impatient Iain arrives in good time. They start to load his sturdy boat; they have done this before often enough to work together smoothly, almost silently. Once she pauses and says 'Kerosene?' But he says that he and Dougie took 60 litres out the week before.

Finally, he starts the engine in neutral, climbs up onto the quay and unties the bow warp. He tells her to put the wheel down hard and she does; the nose of the little boat swings out towards the harbour mouth; he unloops the stern rope, drops it into the boat, jumps gracefully down after it himself and is at the wheel in a single practiced flowing movement. They run out, over the bar and into the open sea.

Depending on the weather and the tides, it is about a 45-minute run from the harbour to the island. The little boat smacks into the waves, but it feels more bouncy and cheerful than rough. She goes forward into the well at the bows and stands holding on to the rail, watching for the moment that they clear the headland north of the harbour, and she will get her first sight of the island lifting its cliffs like a beak towards the west. The business of loading had distracted and soothed her but now her urgency returns. She barely looks at the coast or the passing birds, only forward.

After a while Iain calls her and she forces herself to turn, smile and make her way aft to join him in the little wheel house.

Things are not always what they seem. Iain looks like the local boatman; indeed he is the local boatman, but he also has a PhD in psychology from a Russell League university down in England. He had told them about it one drunken evening at the Research Centre about four years ago. It had been Chen's first year and he had hated it. He was good at the work, and probably now was confident enough to get on with it to the point of enjoying it, but that first summer had been appalling for him: he was scared of the northern light, cold too much of the time and darkly baffled by everyone's enthusiasm. His beautiful self-effacing manners had really not been helpful in the strange enforced intimacy. She had suggested tentatively once that he go back to the mainland, but he had been both angry and hurt. Iain had come out on his regular supply run and had stayed over. Quite suddenly, and in no apparent context, he had turned to Chen and said, 'My thesis was on 'home', on love-of-place, oikophilia we called it. What makes a particular place or topography home, necessary to someone, and why. Just accept this is not yours, and you'll be fine.' There had been a sudden surprised pause, and then he had gone on, told them very briefly about his work, and finally said, 'As a psychologist I'd want to ask why people chose to research particular things. With me it became obvious. I learned I couldn't really live anywhere else except here. I completed the thesis, had a breakdown and came home. I've not been off the outer isles since. Hope I never have to.' He took a slug of whisky and added, 'Of course the really weird ones aren't people like me, with our own language, or own music and our own rather particular landscape. I was kind of interested in the people who find 'home' somewhere they have never been before, that they have no roots in, no story, might go all their lives and never find it, but they do – a sort of instant recognition of here.' And he gave her a straight, clean look. He had barely ever mentioned his past again.

Now he pours tea from a thermos; smiles, looks comfortable in his body, in his boat. The headland drops into the sea. Beyond it the island appears, whole, shapely, welcoming. She lifts the binoculars from her chest, holds them to her face and scans the air above the cliffs.

She is home.

They reverse the loading process, getting everything up onto the jetty and then Iain goes off in search of the trolley, and she walks over to the low building, walking round the inside, resting her hand on the long table, opening the window of her bedroom, checking. Then she goes back out. Iain is already at work stacking the boxes onto the trolley and she joins him.

It takes three loads to get everything into the centre; the smaller boxes on the table and others sitting around on the floor. She thinks Iain will leave now, but he does not. They start to sort everything out. Kitchen area, bedrooms, work space. Iain asks sometimes where he should put something.

He hefts up a small solid cardboard box marked 'FRAGILE'. It has been ripped open and the lid stuck down again.

'What about this?' he asks.

She glances up from her knees beside the sink where she is putting away several bottles of washing-up liquid. 'Oh, put it beside the computer for now. It's the sat-navs.'

'The whats?'

'Satellite navigation thingies. But tiny. The idea is we put them on the skuas and then we can follow them, know where they are, all the time.'

'I thought that was what your computer chips did.' He had always followed the work, in a mildly curious sort of way.

'Well they do, but only when the birds get back. You know, we have to find the individuals, get the chips back off them, download them. And even then they aren't that accurate. These new ones, we will be able to pinpoint them, now, at any given instant.'

'So...?'

'Well the European Fishery people who are paying for them think they can use them to see which fishing boats are dumping catch illegally, against the quota regulations. Skuas, you know, follow fishing boats; they're carrion feeders and it is much less effort for them to take dumped fish than go forcing gannets to give up theirs or just hoping for some dead ones to come bobbing along on the surface. Well obviously it works, because they sorted out dumping in the North Sea and so the skuas went to Portugal – and now we know they are making the effort to go all the way south to Africa. So the plan is that if they know exactly where the skuas are they can match that to where the individual boats are, because they have sat nav anyway, and then they can board and inspect... Skuas as policemen.'

'Hard to imagine bonxies that way,' he says grinning. 'They're more like pirates.'

She grins back, but she is really interested in this and pushes on. 'And for me, from my own point of view, I'm not so interested in dumping, what I am interested in is migration patterns. And – do you remember – the chips work by recording the hours of sunshine, so you can tell the latitude the bird was at on a given date? But the thing is they can't tell you anything useful at the equinoxes.'

'Why?'

'If the days and nights are the same length across the whole hemisphere, you can't get a latitude reading, can you? Equi-nox. Equal nights – and days of course.'

He thinks about it and then smiles.

'That's fine for the Fishery people, but not for me,' she goes on, 'The vernal equinox is exactly when migratory sea birds are migrating. So, at the very moment I want to know most what they're up to, they disappear. Vanish somewhere between winter and summer. But these new things – they'll let me watch them, daily, in real time. They cost an arm and leg mind you – I could only get twelve – they were supposed to come last year, but they arrived too late.'

'Cool,' he says, putting the box on the table. 'Deep magic. Can I look?'

'Sure.' She does not look round, busy with her cupboard. It takes a few moments for his stillness and silence to register with her. She crosses the room to where he is standing, rigid, looking into the box. His right hand is shaking slightly, a just visible tremor.

There should be twelve little boxes in the bigger box. There are only eleven, and a tidy square well where one is missing. She stares at him. At last he draws a shuddering breath and says,

'You ringed him.'

She stares at him.

'You're spying on him. He won't like it. Helen, be careful.'

She goes on staring. Then blushes, looks away. She

cannot pretend he has not spoken.

'How did you know?'

'Mine's a Selkie,' he says, 'a seal woman. Much more standard. Normal... well, relatively. But that's how I know.'

He seems to think that is enough, and she does not know how to ask the questions she wants to hear the answers to. After a few moments she leaves the table, goes out the door and walks down to the tide line. There is a rack of kelp, bobbing close along the rocks. She looks at it.

She has spied on him and he will not like it.

She tries to feel embarrassed, but fails. She looks back towards the low corrugated iron roof of the field centre, sitting in its green grass bowl under the jagged rocks. After a bit Iain comes out of the door, walks down and stands beside her. Together they watch the gentle rocking of the tangled strands of seaweed. Eventually he says quietly,

'I'm sorry. I shouldn't have spoken.

'No,' she said, 'You were kind. Thank you.' Then after a pause she smiles and says, 'It's all right,' and then 'it is all right.' And suddenly it is, it very much is. Her heart rises, singing in the wind. She turns towards him and very briefly, sweetly he hugs her. They go back into the Centre and continue with their chores.

Later she starts to get fidgety. When he notices he says it is time for him to be going. She does not argue. She accompanies him to the jetty, but finds herself glancing up towards the cliff top.

'Don't worry,' Iain says, 'he won't have come in last night.'

'How do you know?'

'Not on the Sabbath.' he says blandly. 'He'll be an island boy.'

They both laugh.

'Thoir an aire dhut fhèin,' he says. 'I'll come out before

the end of the week. Take care of yourself. Agus turas math dhut. Tha mi 'n dòchas gun còrd e riut.'

As soon as she has waved him off, while she can still hear the chug of the engine and pick out his head in the wheelhouse, she turns, zips her jacket and walks up beyond the buildings, following a worn track across the grass. She starts climbing, trying to ignore her winter lack of fitness. The path zigzags up the ever steeper hillside. After about fifteen minutes and panting, she breaks out onto the flat short grass at the top of the island and turns west towards the sunset. At the edge of the cliff she sits cross-legged staring down into the cove; the sharp rocks at the very bottom are white frilled with small breaking waves. The shelves where the gulls nest are still grey with last year's mess. Below her she can see two shags flying low on the water and suddenly a gannet, powerful and lovely, sweeps across her line of vision. She sits very still and waits.

Something has changed. She has ringed him. He does not know and he will not like it. He must not find out.

The western sky is bright but there are clouds over the sun so she can see out towards America. There is nothing else before that.

He comes on the last breath of the day, on the turning of the tide. She sees him first against the light, in silhouette. He comes in straight and fast. She sits tall and stretches out her arms, only slightly wider than his wing span. He is huge and strong, blotting out the sea, the view, her thoughts, everything. He crashes down on her, his webbed feet splaying, grinding into her thighs; his massive beak ramming into her neck, bruising painfully, unbearable, necessary, joyful. His beak is very hard; his feathers thick and soft; his body undernourished but fierce against her breasts – wiry, tough, greedy after his long journey. She folds herself around him. He struggles and then softens. He is so beautiful.

'Bonxie,' she croons.

'M'eudail, tha mi dhachaigh,' he says, 'dhachaigh bhon mhuir.'

She is like a gannet, lovely, graceful, strong. He will harry her, kidnap her, force her to regorge, vomit up her hard-won freedom in the real world. She will scarcely be safe.

She does not care.

'Tha e dhachaigh.' She is home. They are together.

He is a fisherman of souls. Her Bonxie boy.

Rapunzel Revisited

There is a story — no hardly that, there is a ghost, a legend of a story that when her king had died and her children were grown, Rapunzel returned to her tower, for she had found, despite the delights of Court, that she had come to miss the sounds of silence, the wind swinging in from the sea and the birds singing before the day's dawn. And she lived there until she was old.

NOTHING CHANGES.

NOTHING HAS changed. Still the river spreads out into the sand and the tide rises and falls; still the shore is half hidden by the standing grasses in which the wind moves softly; still the village is half hidden in the trees and the little path comes winding out towards me. Still the sea is a soft grey smudge half a mile away and the estuary drifts down towards it. The first morning I saw what I took to be a curlew on flight against the soft morning clouds, bubbling its loud musical song as it flew; and then I realised I could not see its feet trailing behind it and knew it was a whimbrel. And when I knew I remembered how the whimbrel in the air moves its wings faster, less like a lumbering gull, and I was happy. I have not seen a whimbrel singing on the wing as it passes for a long, long time.

Nothing has changed. The windows stand as they always did; deep-bayed curving round with the round walls. The room was ready, waiting. The mirror hangs where the mirror hung and the little brass bed which was too small for the two of us is now too small for me alone.

My embroidery frame is still, is again, on the little marquetrie table by the western window so that the last of the evening light will shine and, as it grows too dark to set my stitches, I can still, or again, watch the distant lights in the village come on and prickle the dusk. Now on the road beyond the village, I can see the bright tiger eyes of cars as they swoop round the long bend and descend the hill into the valley; I can see the red glow of their backward glances too; of their passing out of the village and away to the big wide world which I have left behind. But I climbed and descended that curved path so often in my childhood dreams that it does not seem strange to see the animals of the night do it now.

My writing table stands once more where it always stood in front of the eastern window so that I can record my dreams in the pale wash of dawn before the sun comes up, spreading the brightness that dries them away and turns my thoughts to the day ahead and the hopes of the future. My dream notebook is covered now in a highly wrought pattern of pinks and greens but, to tell the truth, I write little in it because I do not have many dreams. Perhaps I do not dream because I have no desires, or perhaps because I have no conflicts. I have not yet decided. Instead, in a different, more chastely designed notebook, I keep detailed records of the birds I see and the cloud patterns over the estuary and the maze of molehills nightly renewed on the green salt sward below the window. No botany, of course, because that needs close up viewing, would require me to go down and out and scrabble in the fields and woods: I prefer ornithology now because the birds come to me, or rather pass by about their own business, as I watch them.

The blue velvet chair in which the princess curls up to read romances, and looks out from in her romantic daydreams, is still beside the south-facing window, with its lower sill and its enormous view over the reed marsh and the sand dunes. Of course, I never was a princess; my parents were humble and slightly criminal members of the agricultural working class, although my dear husband kept this a well-guarded secret. But every small girl who curls up in a blue velvet winged armchair with silk cushions and reads romances is a princess – and so, since nothing changes, is every middle-aged woman; especially one who was brought up by a Witch.

And the northern window. Can I truly say that nothing changes, that nothing has changed? The wide sill is there still, the casement fitted to the inner wall, not the outer one as the others are; the darker view of the winding path from the village, approaching through the pine trees; the bramble bushes still grow roundabout if I lean out far enough to look down. That has not changed. Yesterday as I looked up from my reading and saw there were three butterflies dancing in the embrasure as they used to dance, dark red against the pale grey stones. But.... but... I have let them put in a wrought iron ladder; we did our best, my architect and I; it is a beautiful ladder designed like a vine, so that you can climb up to the window, or I suppose, I could climb down to the ground, treading leaves and bunches of grapes. They call it a fire-escape and are happy for my safety, but I know that is not why I did it. I cheated. For although my hair is still long, indeed it will still tumble the twenty ells to the ground – and I know this because practically the first thing I did when I returned here was to unwind it and test it – in the last few years it has started to feel brittle. I do not think it has the bouncy toughness of youth, and I am afraid it might snap; I do not want to be reminded of Him falling, falling and crying out like a bird in pain, a baby bird falling from its nest squawking – that is no way to remember one's hero.

Or perhaps it is just vanity, my one gesture of regret for my departing youth, that I should not have, daily, to test my one claim to fame and immortality; I was the woman up whose pure golden hair her lover could climb to a secret chamber of delight. And to be honest there is another reason, not disconnected with this vanity: I have the most agonising arthritis in my neck and shoulders. My doctor cannot understand it. Osteoporosis, he mutters, a common symptom of women of a certain age, that is my age; eat more bananas and take replacement hormones. But why your neck, he asks, as such complaints usually affect joints which have been overused. Like most doctors, he is not really asking me so I do not have to tell him; and this amuses me. The ladder is the price I pay for my amusement, for my vanity and for my ineradicable female concern for the safety and comfort of others. In any order that feels appropriate. But it is not quite true to say that nothing has changed.

The Witch has changed too, although not very much, not as much as I expected.

When I first planned to come back here I was worried about the Witch. I did not want a servant, at my beck and call, for then nothing would be the same. My Witch was never my servant – she was not my servant, nor my mother. She came and went of her own choosing and yet she chose, each morning, to bring me porridge in a little red bowl, to bring it so swiftly through the pine forest that it was still steaming hot when she arrived at the tower, the brown sugar on the top only beginning to melt into golden pools, still crispy in the middle, and the thick cream still floating in the middle of the porridge and erupting up round the inner rim of the bowl. She came and went of her own choosing, and yet she chose each evening to take up the whalebone comb which still sits on the shelf below the mirror and comb out my hair. The songs of the whales, who call their lovers across the grey-green oceans of the earth, sang through each golden strand of my golden hair, and she would comb, comb, comb the twenty ells of gold and singing, like the whales, would braid it up again.

> Over and under, in and out,
> under and over, out and in,

Rapunzel, Rapunzel,
I'm combing your hair.

But she had gone, long years ago, to wherever it is that Witches go after their work is done and I was worried.

I did need a Witch and I did not want a servant. One of the problems with Witches, the useful sort as much as the wicked ones, is that even if you are a queen and a princess, you cannot require their services. That much I have learned from life. Desire may conjure up a lover, or a child, or a quest; but Witches come and go about their own business and not even dire need and the exhaustion of your own resources will compel them. It is as chancy as the behaviour of a single particle in a sunbeam and many of the most deserving women have had to manage without, while Cinderella, for example, who never lifted a finger to help herself, had no difficulties. I had treated my Witch brutally and ungratefully, and had assumed it my duty to do so. And now I needed one badly, even though I was well past the usual age, so of course I was worried.

I need not have been, of course. There is a tendency to assume that Witches have to be older than their Princesses, but my new Witch is as young as my daughter. She does not know she is a Witch, she thinks she is a health visitor and she bounces up the ladder with youthful enthusiasm, radiant good health and a mild excess of jollity which might irritate me if it did not so remind me of my first Witch bustling through the forest at dawn. She brings me my shopping and my post and massages my poor neck and shoulders for me and she brushes my hair because it becomes harder and harder for me to get my arms up to do the job. She waxes it too to protect it against its own brittleness, rubbing in the wax down all twenty ells and then wrapping it up in hot towels that she heats in her microwave. I know she is a Witch because she protects my privacy and does not believe in replacement hormones, but in hot wax and warm towels.

I know she is a Witch for another reason too: I have seen her fly. When I came back I brought a telescope with me so that I could watch the stars and the birds feeding on the water line. Because of the pain in my neck I brought a refracting telescope. A refracting telescope has a lens with a mirror inside that turns the thing you are looking at at right angles to the sight-tube, so that you can look without having to sit on the floor and bend your head back. One summer morning I scanned the telescope along the distant bays where the white, bright water was meeting the bright, white sky – not at anything but for my own pleasure, randomly, asking the world what it would give me as gift, for the brightness of the sunshine and the glory of the silence – and I saw my young witch, flying in the air, cavorting naked, splashing sunlight from her wild dance, skimming low along the water line. I stared amazed and delighted, knowing why she protected my privacy – because it matched her own secrecy. I had forgotten, in my delight, that a refracting telescope reverses the image, left to right and top to bottom like a magic mirror, she was running and dancing on the beach really, but it was a magic moment and I knew she was a Witch and believe still that had I not been looking she might indeed have been flying as the whimbrel flies, not slow and lumbering like a gull, but swift and true in the sunshine.

Refraction distorts the image, but does not thereby make it less true. I chose to come back here because it was the only place I had direct experience of. It has been my story to see the world only through refractors, and never to experience it directly. When I was a child I sat in my blue velvet chair and learned everything through images, through books, through stories. Only out of the windows could I see the world; only through the climbings up and down of the Witch and of the Prince could I have contact with the outside world. But here I thought, here there was my real experience: here, untrammelled by the refractions, I could hear the sounds of silence, the wind swinging in from the sea and the birds singing before the day's dawn.

I came because there were questions that I wanted to answer.

Did I love my Witch or hate her?
Did she imprison me or protect me?
Did she love me or hate me?
Was she a good Witch or a wicked one?
Why did my parents give me away so lightly when they had, so they say, wanted me for so long? Did they love me or hate me?
Did I love the Prince for himself or for the love he gave me?
Did I ever make a choice, or did I move with the tides, as the reeds and the river do? As the reeds and river must?
As all the stories must?

But it does not work. I find that I do not, as I had planned, brood obsessively on my past, but rather that my past comes creeping in to shape my present. My past demands a Witch; and I peer through my telescope and find one.

The stories still come between me and my seeing, me and my hearing. Long ago I read that in a country far away to the south they believe that the Milky Way is a river of stars that connects in the deep sea with the rivers of the land, and that the two nourish each other. Now I cannot look at the estuary under the light of the moon without joining it, far away out there with the river in the sky. The story has fixed my seeing.

Long ago I read that in the cold icelands in the north where the geese go for the summer, they believe that twins are salmon-babies; their souls are the souls of the great fish and their hearts have the same playfulness and longing to be travelling that the salmon have. Now I cannot watch the fishermen go out to their nets at low tide and carry in their catch without my heart being caught in anxiety for my own twins, and I fear that they have slipped back into their true bodies and have been caught in the nets themselves. The story has fixed my seeing.

So it is impossible for me to shape my future, although that is what I came to do. I have been the child, and the beloved and the queen and the widow. I have come to a place where I need a new story, a new way of seeing and I am so entangled in the old ones, unbrushed and unbraided, that I cannot let down my hair and haul up a future.

The world is refracted through the lense of my life and I cannot see it natural and undistorted. Perhaps instead of coming back here I would have done better to go travelling. I have read that in the jungle you can see dancing clouds of tiny yellow and white butterflies. They hover over the places where turtles come out of the water to sun themselves on fallen logs; the butterflies gather, like confetti in a breeze, to sip the tears from the turtles' eyes. I would have liked to have seen that: and as the pain of my past joys bends my neck forward and I retreat into my tower like a shell, I wonder if this is the story for my old age when my cheerful Witch dances up the ladder to comfort me?

So, in a way, it is true that nothing has changed. But I have changed.

It is, and you were fairly warned, not a story, only the ghost, the legend of a story. There is no plot, no narrative. Nothing happens. But still the wind swings in from the sea and the birds sing before the day's dawn; and still she listens to the sounds of silence which she had missed, despite the delights of the Court. Still she finds witches and whimbrels to enchant her days and still she looks through the refracting lens of all the stories to try and find her own truth, her own story: The story of the woman who has been child and beloved and queen and has finished with all those tasks and must now try to learn to be herself.

The Swans

THE YOUNG QUEEN LIES in her great bed and listens. In her own silence she has become attuned to the silence of the night, so she can hear the huge silent spinning of the stars and the soft footfalls of cats on the prowl. Her newborn boy-child in the carved and gilded cradle breathes silently through his first night.

The Young Queen has been silent long enough to hear properly. She hears the quiet, malevolent steps of the Old Queen, her husband's mother, climbing the winding stair, and approaching the royal birth chamber along the cold passageway. The Young Queen closes her eyes so she cannot see, but she cannot close her ears. She hears the door-latch lift and the candle flames shimmer in the new draught. She hears the Old Queen walk to the cradle and the whispered creak as the baby is lifted out. She hears the Old Queen's slippers turn on the stone floor and – nearly as silently as the cats – come towards the bed. She knows the Old Queen is standing beside her, the child on one arm and the small bowl of goat's blood in her other hand.

'I know you are awake,' says the Old Queen, very softly.

The Young Queen opens her eyes and the two of them look straight at each other. Almost, perhaps, nearly, they smile. The Young Queen respects the Old Queen; she even admires her.

The Young Queen knows that she herself would not rest easy if her son, if any of her three sons, came home one day with a half-naked but beautiful woman-child who would not speak. A woman whose eyes proved her understanding and her feeling, but who never spoke, never laughed, never sang. 'Witchcraft', she would have feared, 'magic things'; and the Old Queen fears them too. Sometimes, as the Old Queen does always, the Young Queen despises the King, her husband, because he loves a woman about whom he knows nothing – a woman who never speaks, never laughs, never sings, never cries out in joy or pain, even in the night in the great royal bed.

'I know you are awake,' says the Old Queen into the Young Queen's silence.

'Look,' says the Old Queen, 'Look at me. Once again, I am going to steal this child away. I am going to smear your mouth with goat's blood and tell them you have eaten him. This will be the third time. This time they will believe me. You will be burned for a witch.'

The Young Queen closes her eyes.

`Call, go on, call out,' says the Old Queen, 'shout, just once, and they'll come running. I have the baby and the bowl of blood. Proof. They'll burn me instead.'

And I will have won, says her silence, which the Young Queen can hear, I will have defeated you and your everlasting silence.

The Old Queen places the bowl on the table beside the bed and dabbles her fingers in it. The Young Queen feels the Old Queen's hand warm on her mouth and chin; she can smell the salt-sweet goat's blood. Then she feels the air stretch between her lips and the heavy-ringed fingers, hears the Old Queen shift the child on her arm, pick up the bowl, turn and leave the room.

The Young Queen lies quite still. There is blood on her mouth and blood between her legs but she does not attempt to wipe either away. Silently the night turns, turns towards the morning and the Young Queen waits until there is light enough to get up and continue her sewing.

High on the shoulder, in the pass between the mountains, the tarn holds the water from the steep hills above in its peaceful arms. This plateau is the watershed; two tiny streams flow out at either end of the tarn, but it itself is perfectly still. The dawn comes slowly. The stars fade and the black sky turns indigo. Details emerge colourless out of the darkness. The sky changes: indigo, grey, cream. The view opens away mysteriously: far, far below, southwards, the river twists and loops silver down to the bay; far, far below, northwards, the forest stretches dark and dense into the distance.

The sky changes: grey, cream, peach. The higher mountains to the west catch the first sun, a splash of brightness like blood. Over the eastern cliff two buzzards float. The moth-markings of their under-wings are lit suddenly by the new sun, tawny gold as they ride the air.

The sky changes: cream, peach, pale, palest blue. There is no wind. The tarn is milky white. But when the seven swans lumber up out of the reed bed and lurch clumsy, bulky, awkward on their stubby feet to the pebble shore, then the surface of the tarn is not white but silver because the swans are white. They take to the water and are changed, graceful, wild and silent. Whiter than dreams, their beaks red-orange, with black knobbed nostrils and eyes, they drift so, not rippling the shining silver. The sun rises. A sudden shocking gold stabs on to the water. The swans swim together, a raft of white, heads curving forward. They turn together, facing northwards, the sun bright on their right flanks.

There is a huge bashing, crashing, splashing din as they lumber, beat their way down the tarn, wings labouring, feet running, kicking on the water. Faster, louder. Then on a breath they are airborne, majestic, powerful, circling as the water falls back into stillness. Above the tarn they form themselves into a wedge, an arrowhead. Together as a single flight they turn north. As they settle into their steady drive, the throbbing music of their wingbeats breaks the silence over the hills and forest.

The Young Queen sits near the window to catch the first light. As soon as she can see what she is doing, she picks up her sewing. Her stitches are tiny, delicate and placed with exquisite care. The middle finger of her right hand is roughened and calloused from the pricks and pins of her long task. Even after all her years of practice it is still difficult to sew the dry white starwort petals with the short threads of yellow sepal. She cannot hurry this work. She does not hurry, even though she is fairly certain that she will not have time now to complete the last of the shirts.

The sky changes: grey, cream, peach. She does not wipe the blood from her lips. As the sky brightens she hears the King come up the stairs. There is a knock on her door but no pause before the latch is lifted. She lowers her head over her sewing. The King and his close council come into the room, standing solemn, stern, strangely calm. The King crosses the floor and glances into the empty cradle. He looks at her and she raises her head to meet his eyes. She sees his horror and sadness. He sees how beautiful she is, and how serene. Tears spring in both their eyes, spill over the lashes, run down their cheeks, but they say nothing. For once, he has joined her in her silence. They look at each other for a long moment. Then he turns, and all the court with him, and blunders from the room.

The sky changes: cream, peach, pale palest blue. At last, she rises and looks out the window southward over the enormous forest. She is not frightened of the forest though many people are. She has wandered there by moonlight from April through to June gathering starwort, the white flowers nodding on their tall straggling stems. Today there is nothing to be seen but the dark of the forest and the pale blue sky. She leans forward over the casement and looks down on the courtyard where there are men busy building a pile of tarred wood around a stake, a bonfire to burn the witch. The tower is high so they look foreshortened, unreal, like insects scuttling. She walks to a chest on the far side of the room, and opens it and takes out the six shirts she has finished. She goes back to her seat, lays the shirts in a tidy pile beside her and picks up the unfinished shirt. She starts sewing again, stitching carefully, patiently, while she waits.

It is clear that she cannot walk down the spiral staircase. Only yesterday she had a child. One of the guards carries her. His arms are strong and her head lies on his shoulder. She has one arm round his neck and on the other she carries the seven starwort shirts, even the last, the unfinished one which has no left sleeve, because there is no more time. They have a strange, old-fashioned scent, a smell of summer and hops and mown grass, that soothes her.

At the foot of the tower the young guard puts her down, but she sways and falls against him. He picks her up again and slowly and solemnly carries her across the great courtyard to the pyre they have built for her. She is so beautiful he thinks his heart will break, but when she raises her head he sees the blood still on her mouth and his gorge rises and he puts her down abruptly. She turns away from him and by herself, freely, she clambers up the log pile. At the top she pauses. Now she uses one of the shirts to wipe her face, to wipe away the blood. Then she turns to face the crowd and she is so beautiful that there is silence.

The silence is broken by a pompous lawyer reading a long and pointless document. You cannot kill a Queen or a witch in silence. There has to be some legal process to go through. The law is about words so it is no concern of hers. She wants for him to be done and, while she waits, she thinks. She is sad because she does not want to die. She is sad because she loves the King. She is sad because she has held each of her three children for only a few moments. She is sad because she has not rescued her seven brothers from their enchantment, although she has tried so hard.

The reading finishes. They ask her formally if she has any defence, but they know now she will not speak and so there is a slight blurring of the protocol. Let what must be done be done quickly now. No one likes it and no one will turn back.

The Old Queen is as silent now as the Young Queen. A trumpet is blown. A brand is lit. The smoke rises thick and black against the white walls of the palace; then thinner and whiter against the pale blue sky. Everyone's eyes follow it upwards, then squint into the morning sun. The bearer of the flaming brand starts to march up the courtyard towards the Young Queen on her high pyre.

There is a throbbing song, a dark music in the air and, through the smoke, fast, faster than dreams, there is an arrow-head, a white drive of power and air and wind and the great beating music of the swans' wings and a high shrill cry. And the Young Queen takes the shirts from her left arm with her right hand and tosses them high into the air and each swan, without a break in its onrushing flight, without shifting its place in the wedge, catches up a shirt in its red-orange bill. Sssssssssssssshshshshshs. Is it the hiss of angry swans or of swords swift-drawn from their scabbards as the seven brothers surround their sister? They are swans no more, but the Young Queen's brothers, now set free from their long enchantment. Then there is a peal of laughter like a bell and it is the Young Queen laughing in the arms of the King.

They all live happily ever after. Even the three lost children are found, hidden in the Old Queen's Dower House. The two older ones are happy to meet their happy father and their beautiful mother; the new, tiny one gurgles joyful on her breast. They have learned something from her silence, they never ask why she preferred her brothers to her sons.

The brothers and the King become friends. They hunt and drink and sing together. They all love the Young Queen and are grateful to her. Though the youngest brother walks strangely, lopsided, and grows wild and silent. He has no left arm and from his left shoulder springs a great white wing of power and beauty. But even the youngest brother in a fairy story cannot fly with only one wing.

The Eighth Planet

*We see the eighth planet as Colombus saw America from the shores
of Spain. Its movements have been felt, trembling along the far-
reaching line of our analysis, with a certainty hardly inferior to that
of ocular demonstration.*
– John Herschel, President of the British Association,
son of William Herschel, musician and astronomer,
10 September 1846

IN THE END HE said, quite calmly, at breakfast one morning,
that he thought he would go back to London later that
afternoon: he did not mean for a trip or even a visit, he meant
for good, he meant *Goodbye* and possibly even, *Thank you for
having me.*

I said nothing; I just looked at him and realised with some
deep and abiding sadness that my main emotion was of relief.
He finished his coffee and went upstairs to start packing. I put
on my wellington boots – black, I would like to say, not green
– and walked down to the shop to get the newspaper, and, ah
God, it was a lovely, lovely morning. It was bright and clean
as some days in late March can be, the sky pale blue and the
branches of the hedgerow trees apparently getting fatter,
pregnant with buds that are not yet even palest green, and the
larch wood across the hillside was pink with promise and,
despite my best efforts to tell myself that he was a bastard and
my great love affair had come to a nasty end and everything
was tragic, all I felt was a heart-lifting joy in the sparkly dew

drops and a sweet pleasure at the thought of being alone again.

Even now, I don't really understand why it turned out so horrendous. We went in with such high hopes, the hopes, we thought, of maturity and good sense, no adolescent romantics we; two people with meshing needs and a deep sense of sexual attraction. And for the first couple of months it was wonderful; we even reached the point of talking about selling both our houses and finding somewhere that would be ours. Once in the middle of a snowy night just before Christmas when we had been out, muffled up like children, we had even mentioned the possibility of having a baby — or rather, to be precise, he had said, 'Let's build a snowman. I need to get in practice for when we have a child.' We had started to roll one of those progressive balls that get larger and larger and leave neat black lines weaving about the lawn, but in the end we had gone to bed instead.

And then quite unexpectedly we had gone into a place of hell; of meanness and hatefulness. Never, never have I felt for anyone the hatred, the irresistible hatred, that I felt for him and he for me: a hatred that could not permit a decent withdrawal, that could not even confine itself to scathing, hurtful arguments but erupted into appalling violence that was mutual and savage and unlovely. But was also completely engaging, an eyeball-to-eyeball clash of the whole of two people, locked together like the lovers in Dante's *Inferno*. I, I who had always loathed romanticism, that 'all for love and the world well lost' stuff, I who preferred relationships to be domestic and comfortable and not distracting, who liked my sex civilised and preferred to do the crossword puzzle anyway. So, on top of everything else, there was this deep shame in both of us, and more simply embarrassment that we should see ourselves and each other like this. And for me at least, a complete loss of identity; quite literally I did not know who I was and I had done no work all winter and could not imagine how I thought I was going to pay for that.

And after some months of that, it suddenly went away. There was a great calm after the storm and we looked at each other more in amazement than in anything else; a sort of terrified surprise, kind of Who *is* this, who can have reduced me to such depths? And we were courteous and civil with each other and there was simply nothing there. We even made love with a tenderness and concern for the other's pleasure, and had long and sincere conversations about where and what each of us might do next, and he fixed new shelves for my kitchen and I knitted him a huge Aran sweater, with elaborate and elegant cables up back and front. And now, when we had, so to speak, completed our rest cure, it was time for him to go back to London.

I walked back from the village shop with the newspaper under my arm and a couple of packets of cigarettes in my pocket and recognised that I was making new plans, plans for work and plans for the vegetable garden, even plans for a summer holiday. And that felt so good. I put the newspaper on the kitchen table and called up the stairs to him, and then I went into the garden to pick him some daffodils to take back to his cold flat in London, just as I would have done for any weekend guest. And indeed I started thinking about weekend guests and friends that I had not seen for months, and I could feel something in my lower neck relax, and my feet spread themselves out inside my spacious wellington boots. I went inside and dumped the flowers in a bucket in the back kitchen, took off my boots and padded in my socks to my pinboard to find the train timetable.

While I was standing there he came downstairs and I noticed with an abstract pleasure how beautiful he still was, conscious that I had not noticed this for weeks, even months. He had been one of the most beautiful undergraduates of our year when I had first known him twenty years ago. A wild glamour that had somehow never gone away, not even now he was cleaner and tidier and richer than any of us could ever have dreamed of. Whereas I, it would have to be said, had not aged so well, and indeed was sloppier, dirtier and cosier than I would have dared to be then, when even my uniform jeans had about them a circumspection and a willingness to be checked out and inspected by anyone who cared. We had been in one of those Trotskyite groupings, those joyfully puritanical, fragmenting, shifting, passionate student groups in the late sixties; not the guitars and marijuana sorts, although actually we did lots of both of these, more the beer and theory until three in the morning kind, our radical paths crisscrossing for a while, an alliance forming between us, then a friendship. And anything was possible in those giddy optimistic times when the mornings had edges so sharp you could cut yourself on the daylight. I had even slept with him a couple of times, before other things intervened.

Later, I had got married and divorced and I met him again last year at one of those dinner parties in London where people envy each other their success while feeling slightly guilty about their own; friendship networks so old and intimate that the difficulties and differences can collapse into wild mirth at an instant, or can flare into fights which, however vicious at the time, will not actually change anything nor prevent the same people coming together again pretty soon, at an identical but different pine kitchen table where everyone tries to keep secret to themselves that they wished the wine was a little better. Property prices and psychoanalysis are mentioned shyly as perhaps our parents mentioned sex, but once on the table, so to speak, it turns out that we are all enormously knowledgeable. And I do not wish to sound so mean, because they are my friends and indeed I am one of them and would not be otherwise. And we are all anti-Thatcherites and those that have them struggle desperately to keep their children within the state school system, and see the all-too-frequent failures of others to succeed as being somehow like a rather nasty disease – compassion and sorrow the appropriate response rather than that clear bell-like anger we could all touch so easily once upon a time.

It was actually quite odd that he and I had not met in this way at any time before. We had that night, I remember, a conversation about who had actually believed in 1969 that The Revolution was real and immediate, and half-sheepishly both of us admitted a complete and profound faith, and had smiled wryly at each other, though whether at our once naivety or our failure to live up to so fine and pure a commitment was not so totally obvious. But it had been, you must understand, a credo, a way of living, which had after all been sincere and which had also been expensive to abandon and left us fretful still. Later I drove him home, since Hackney is basically on the way to Ipswich, and since he does not own a car and it was late. And outside his charming Victorian terraced artisan's cottage (through lounge, two beds, kitchen/diner, bathroom, gas-fired central heating, tastefully refurbished preserving many period features; I know how mean and catty I am and to punish myself have to admit that my cottage has a thatched roof), we encountered one of those odd surges of pure desire that are entirely mutual and he said to me, 'We have unfinished business, you and I.' And whatever that had been, it was now at least well and truly finished.

So I could smile at his beauty and, indeed, at him, not without some considerable pleasure when he came down the stairs into my kitchen. He had the newspaper in his hand and an apologetic grin on his face.

He asked, 'What time is the late train?'

I inspected the timetable and told him. 'Why?' I asked.

'We could see Neptune tonight. With the telescope.' He flapped the paper gently.

He would not ask to stay another night. I would have resented it bitterly if he had. But he would very much like to see Neptune with the telescope. It was an odd thing about the telescope. It had belonged to the uncle of mine who had left me the cottage and had been waiting along with other treasures when I arrived. I had kept it only because it was a very beautiful object, with lovely brass bits and pieces: there is something extraordinarily lovely to me in Victorian scientific instruments, along with clocks and musical boxes, where the desire that something should work perfectly is not made a reason for not having it look wonderfully wrought. Properly speaking, it is probably like the crinoline, merely an example of conspicuous consumption, a public way of saying, Look how much I can afford to spend, but in its presence I could never focus on that but only on the pleasure that looking at it gave me. I never used it for anything, indeed found it well-nigh impossible to see anything through it, even the larch trees across the hill, but he loved it functionally. At the golden beginning of our relationship when we had first come down to the cottage, he had fallen on it with joy and arrived the next time with a small pile of star charts and books. Back in the autumn he had spent hours looking through it, while I had curled on the sofa enjoying the anticipation of lust, the mounting excitement of waiting. He would try to show me what he was looking at sometimes, but proximity and darkness were usually too much for us. I had not proved myself an adept at amateur astronomy.

'Is that special?' I asked him now.

'Special enough for the late train.' After a short pause he said, 'Please.'

'All right then,' I said, 'I can drive you to the station after that.'

Much later, when we had had tea and were waiting for the darkness, he said, 'I'll tell you something about Neptune that you may not like. It disproves the whole thing about learning coming from experience, theory being grounded on what actually is. They discovered it by pure theory.'

I asked him what he meant.

'In 1781 William Herschel became the first person in history to discover a planet, Uranus. He discovered it as you might expect, as most things are discovered, by well informed accident and good luck, by looking, just by looking at everything through his telescope, which he had made himself because he couldn't afford to buy one. He looked and looked and thought about what he saw and he discovered a planet – planets don't twinkle, you see, and under sufficient magnification they show a disk not a point of light. Well, after he had found it, other astronomers tried reasonably enough to plot its orbit, but wherever they thought it ought to be it wasn't. So they worked out, in total abstract, that it was being pulled out of its expected orbit by the gravity of another invisible planet, somewhere out there, somewhere beyond the known limits of the sun's cosmic system. Somewhere so far out that you could not see it with the naked eye. And in principle it should be possible to work out exactly where it was. So this young mathematician called John Couch Adams did just that in 1845. Sort of typical academe, he could not get anyone to look for it for him. Some Frenchman called Urbain Leverrier worked it out too. So they knew it was there; they knew it was there, and exactly where theoretically before they found it.'

I may not need to mention that he was a teacher of extraordinary verve and energy, whose lectures were well attended and whose books, given their academic abstraction, sold remarkably well. He loved to impart information like this.

And I, I loved being told stories like this. He had known that too when he had said I might not like it. That was a tease, because he knew I was a sucker when it came to this sort of incident. I pushed him for all the details he knew; I imagined poor John Adams trekking around the astronomers of Britain saying, 'There it is, there it is, look, look it's your job to look', and no one believing him enough to bother to get into their observatories and look for it. I find it odd how little people ever seem to want to detect things they're meant to detect. Like the Yorkshire Ripper, for example. How on the available evidence could they have failed to find Sutcliffe? You collect all the evidence and then you almost wilfully fail to act on it.

Only amateurs, lovers, in their chambers on Baker Street, half sozzled with cocaine, actually want to solve mysteries. So I said, 'Tell me, tell me.'

And sitting by the fireplace in my little cottage with a big mug of tea between his hands and his lovely high-boned face turned away from me and towards the flames, he told me more things.

He told me that Neptune has two moons: one is tiny and called Miranda, and the other is huge and called Triton; and Triton is the only object in the cosmic universe that revolves in the opposite direction. Of all the planets and all their satellites, only Triton has the imagination to spin backwards. He told me that Neptune has not rings, like Saturn and Jupiter and Uranus but arcs, little bits of broken-up ring, material all that way away striving to turn itself from a strip into a clump – matter that desires to be a satellite. He told me that Neptune is a liquid, its surface entirely covered by water. He told me that at the bottom of this ocean, which functions as a blanket, it is so hot that the methane at its core is perhaps breaking up into carbon atoms and hydrogen atoms and the carbon is being pressed into diamond crystals. Far away, beyond the furthest seeing of the naked eye, there is the jewel-encrusted underwater cavern that the ancients dreamed of for their sea god, Neptune.

And this they knew from pure theory alone. Even Voyager 2 has not yet travelled long enough or far enough to see Neptune in any detail.

And in the freezing night we turned off the lights and he looked through the telescope, referring at first to the newspaper and then to his huge space atlas. And suddenly he gave a tiny shiver of pleasure and I knew he had found it. He looked for a moment and then fixed the telescope, twiddling one of the elegant brass knobs effortlessly and without taking his eye away from the lens.

'Come and see,' he said, stretching out one arm and tucking

me into the fold of his body, as I had so many times been tucked before. But his energy was flowing not towards me but towards the whole dense sky. I put my eye against the optic and at first could see nothing, then I could see too much, a million too many stars, a great war in heaven, and I was almost terrified. And keeping his arm round me, warm and gentle, he told me very quietly what to look for, how to find Neptune and suddenly there it was: a tiny distant pale bluish disc floating out there. It did not twinkle or waver. I was amazed. Even if I never saw him again, he would have given me this gift, this sight of a new world known, discovered and created by theory.

'Thank you,' I said with real pleasure.

'No, thank you,' he said, and I turned within his arms and we exchanged a kiss so pure and tender that I have never known anything like it.

It was so perfect a moment that it became immediately imperative that he should catch the train. He pushed the lens cover over the telescope and took the stairs two at a time in his energetic determination to get his bags down and into the car. I helped him, not even bothering to say we had plenty of time. There was a sort of panic and unreasonableness about our haste which seemed appropriate to us both; but as soon as we were both in the car I realised that I had forgotten to give him the flowers I had picked that morning. I leapt out again and ran back in the empty cottage. When I saw the telescope still standing on its tripod at the window I knew I had to give it to him – not the flowers after all, but that. I folded it up and packed it into its leather box. He came to the door, impatient to be gone, and saw what I was doing. He didn't even question me, it was so right. He said thank you once again and then came over and squatting together on the floor, we did up the leather straps and brass buckles with infinite and delicate care. Then together we carried it out to the car and laid it on the back seat. Then we both scrambled back into the car and belted off; I knew I was over-revving the engine, and that it was foolish to take the bend by the old mill stream at such a pace, but there was a desperate compulsion about it. I wanted him out of my life, right then and there. And I could feel him beside me wanting the same thing.

The silence in the car felt painfully oppressive. I heard myself jabbering suddenly, endless words pumping out. I said, 'Now I'll tell you a story, or at least a thought, about Neptune. If it was discovered in 1846 there is a wild appropriateness about that: just two years, enough time for it to sneak into public consciousness, before 1848; and Neptune was the god of revolutions, of storms, of raising new worlds out of the ocean deeps. Homer says that when Neptune issued from the sea and crossed the earth in three strides, the mountains and the forests trembled. He was the god who was always restless and invented the horse as a symbol of war and slaughter. So maybe there really is something in astrology.'

He laughed. I drove slower. The twistings of the country lane had, almost without our noticing it, imposed some sort of calmness on my driving. The desperate urgency evaporated, flowing off into the dark night around us.

I asked him, 'How did you get into stars, anyway? It does seem a rather improbable hobby for the bright young scientific socialist.'

'Oh, well,' he replied, apparently laughing, `scientific socialism got all buggered up. You bloody feminists did that, punched holes right through the middle of the fabric of the thing, didn't you? Where else is there for a scientific marxist to go but off to explore new worlds and the further away the better? Like the Levellers after the collapse of the Commonwealth. You take your mysticism to the country and bury it in the mud; I take my science to the skies and bury it in darkness.'

I glanced at him and his beautiful face was tense not just with anger but with pain.

I said, 'You may not believe this, but underneath it all, I don't know how the hell to go about it and I don't live it on the flesh of experience, as I said we ought to, and I'm a fat cat and will greet the Revolution if it comes, with tears for what I'm losing, rather than the more traditional dancing in the streets, but... but I still do believe that the overthrow of capitalism is The Project.'

And he said, 'I know you do. The question is, do I?'

And after a little while longer I said, 'It is sad. I somehow cannot escape the feeling that we all, all of us, all our generation of people, deserved better than we got. And yet we got so much.'

'*Sic transit gloria mundi,*' he said a little peevishly.

'No,' I said, 'that's not what I mean.'

'No,' he said, 'I know it isn't, but I'm bloody well not going to say thank you again. More like the Transit of fucking Venus or something.'

And that was enough of that. So we talked inconsequentially of this and that, friends and acquaintances, gossip and memories. Suddenly he started to tell me about Neptune again. I thought I didn't really want to hear that, but it was better than nothing and we were still a considerable distance from the train station. I half listened as he talked about densities, and gravities, and mass versus size. And suddenly I heard something in his voice, a sharpening, a precision, perhaps even a kind of nervousness, and I knew he was telling me something that was infinitely precious to him. He was telling me about Neptune's vast moon, Triton, whom from his previous description I had assumed to be something of the joker in the pack, eternally revolving backwards against all possible odds. And yes, yes, that was part of it, obviously; but also infinitely no. There's some astronomer in Haiti who spent a great deal of time speculating – both looking at and guessing about – on Triton. Now he said to me, in the apparently enclosed world of the car rushing through the countryside, he said, 'It is a world of chilly oceans, whole oceans of liquid nitrogen. Away out there, those icy oceans coloured red, vivid crimson, by organic matter that we do not yet understand, rocked with tides beyond our moon space, infinitely pulled by a different, extenuated, frail force of gravity, and riding majestic those great rollers, silent because there is no breaking shore, there is no hearer for their thunder, riding the crimson oceans are the stately blue-white icebergs of another place.'

He said all that and I, to my own surprise, said, 'Frozen methane.'

You probably understand by now that we had been trying all these months to be together – it had been an investment of great importance to us both, had taken us both into a new place of self-knowing – and now, too late to be of any use, in that extraordinary and almost casual reversal – my science, his poetry – we almost succeeded. If I had been able, just then, to take both hands off the steering wheel and show him how I had, once, a world away, oh hell, a cosmos away almost, in a small ship, seen the dignified and blue-white icebergs of our own planet, bobbing too gigantic for the word itself, seen them break themselves with a deep gonging sound off the master ice, the glacier ice, and swan-white as their own chosen style, down the great green – oh so green – drift waters of the Arctic Ocean, I think we might even have gone home and tried again. You know, that is the magic of incongruence, where two pieces of the apparently seamless garment of social reality do not quite fit together, and through the unknown gap comes seeping – well, what can I call it? the unexpected, the redemptive, the bizarre but also the welcome – oh well, comes seeping Joy. Like lava from between the dense, privy, immeasurably shifting and dishonest plates of the earth's surface. But you know how it is really too – I was driving; I had responsibilities; there was a sharp bend, concentration-requiring; and then it was too late, or not appropriate, or something. That's the way it goes, all randomly and inexplicably.

As it was, we were both delighted. And we damn nearly missed that train.

Claudia Procula Writes a Letter

My dear Prisca,

'*Quel ennui!*' you will doubtless exclaim receiving yet another letter from your old friend, but believe me, my dear, your tedium is as nothing compared to mine, so you will just have to endure yours, for the sake of those happy days of our childhood. Little did I think then that I would end up with a tiresome husband in some outpost of the Empire with nothing to do but admire my ever-advancing wrinkles and bore my poor friends with vacuous letters.

Nothing has changed since last I wrote, as you will not be surprised to hear, except that we are presently not in the governor's palace in Caesarea Philippi, but in Jerusalem itself, which is, if anything, even worse – especially as we are here for one of their everlasting religious festivals.

You cannot believe the natives here. You might think that some of them would want to enjoy the fruits of civilisation – or at the very least be willing to amuse so influential a lady as myself. But no such luck! They're all intensely solemn and deeply religious, sober, silent and hate us with a deep and joyless sullenness, like sulky boys kept in for the afternoon; and it's worst at festivals like this, when apparently half the native population wants to be in Jerusalem – I can't imagine why, a dirtier, more squalid town would be impossible to imagine, and not even a decent water supply – which is another long story. Do you know our last riot was caused because PP thought that fresh water might be a good idea? He's quite conscientious in his dull little way. Well, of course, it was going to have to be paid for. I really thought their temple chappies would be happy to shell out of their monstrously large revenues for a pretty little viaduct; after all, they're the ones that make money out of Jerusalem's version of religious tourism. Not a bit of it; they all got up on their high horses about Romans stealing temple funds and the next thing you know is the whole city is seething with dirty little men chucking paving stones.

Anyway, be that as it may, nine-tenths of the countryside swarms into this cesspit of a town, and then they all sit around the temple discussing their law and ancient liberties. This festival celebrates some antique intervention of their grim and ferocious God, who they claim brought them freedom from slavery, and gave them this country as their own. They chant interminable songs about it and slaughter thousands of sheep and daub their walls with blood. Very nasty. Not surprisingly the tension mounts. They won't even eat with people who work for us; there's a tangible hostility in the air which would be frightening if they weren't also the most appalling cowards. At least the temple chaps are – they don't want any trouble from their own people since last time, when it was made quite clear to them that if they could not maintain order, then the whole temple would simply be razed to the ground. Still, they don't like it, or us. Needless to say, in this atmosphere, there's a breeding ground for millennial lunatics, petty insurgents, and what PP would call riotous assemblies. Poor little me can't go out of the palace in safety without an armed cohort, and all of them are needed on patrol so I might as well be a prisoner here rather than the wife of the Roman Governor.

We did entertain their sort of king fellow, a nasty little quisling called Herod, to dinner last night. The most vulgar, creepy undersized worm you can't imagine; quite different from his dead Papa, if all one hears is true. Not that he was exactly all sophistication and amiability and culture, but at least he had some style. They say he actually turned down a direct proposition from *La Belle Egyptienne* − yes, Cleopatra herself, although I must say, looking at the son, I don't understand it. Anyway, the present model is not only despicable, he's weak and further confuses the political situation, which is quite deplorable already.

I'll take the risk that the censors won't open a private letter from a distant relation of our great Emperor to a courtier of our esteemed Empress, and tell you frankly that PP is entirely out of his depth. He wants everyone to like him − I can't imagine why − almost as much as he doesn't want a repeat of the last two debacles. Though it would hardly seem to matter, if you ask me, since we must by now have said goodbye to his chances of getting the governorship of Syria. Just my bad luck to be married to the Roman Governor who has been responsible for not one but two of the worst riots this end of the Mediterranean in this decade. Poor lamb, one could almost feel for him, except that his general twitchiness and smarminess towards their authorities seriously curtails my life. Strictly *entre nous*, the strains have reduced his virile Romanity rather drastically but because of his sensitivities towards their local customs and manners, poor little Claudia has to be unspeakably discreet.

I sound disgusting. I'm not surprised I don't hear from you more often − whingeing self-pity collapsing into bad taste does not make for a lively correspondent, does it? But, Prisca, I cannot tell you. It is bad enough to live somewhere where nothing ever happens, but when nothing ever happens in an atmosphere of sullen hatred, it's unbearable. When I think that when we were first married I really believed he would be a maker of history, his name known for all time! You must remember how impressive he was. And now he's earnest, unamusing, and scared in a self-seeking sort of way.

Right at the moment, *par exemple*, there's a whole lot of unease because of this young man from the northern half of the province who's arrived in town. He's rather good looking in a hairy sort of way, and can talk the hind legs off a donkey (oh, yes, I went and took a discreet peek, you know me). He doesn't seem to have any beef about Romans, in fact he seems to ignore us all, although Pontius says there's some half-witted centurion in town who insists that this fellow healed some dying servant of his when they were on duty up-country a year ago. But a couple of days ago, he and his friends nearly caused a riot in the temple itself, and the priests and scribes obviously don't care for him. Well, now they want us to run him in and have him executed, though quite what for they don't seem to know; which is pretty typical. They could at least have cooked up a decent case and let us off the hook. No one can really pretend that claiming to be the Son of God constitutes a capital offence, and what's more, given our esteemed Emperor, one would hardly like to make such a risky suggestion, would one?

It seems perfectly obvious to me that PP should do one of two things – either have the chap arrested and strung up just as quick as he can, or tell these priest types to get lost, and take the consequences. But, oh no, he's got all interested and wants to talk to the man himself, which will be fatal – you wait. I mean it is hardly dignified to get involved in a whole lot of chatter about what constitutes blasphemy; it implies that we have some sort of belief in these outdated local deities. All he needs is a good flogging and being sent home to the countryside. The natives will all disperse at the end of the week, they always do. But PP has got all serious and conscientious about it. To tell the truth, I'm moderately anxious about the whole thing – the people here are so odd, you can never guess how they'll respond to anything. In fact, I pulled a minor deception on my poor old spouse: I sent him a message saying that he should wash his hands of the whole business, because I'd been warned against this Nazarene fellow in a dream – all rubbish of course, but he has got so superstitious recently that I hoped it might work. If I just told him what I thought, he wouldn't pay any attention at all.

But all this is boring. I am sorry. It's not fair of me to use up your precious time moaning like this, especially as you and I can both guess exactly how it will end. Sooner or later there'll be another riot and PP and I will end our days in some gruesome provincial villa in exile, and I'll still have no one to amuse me.

Oh Prisca, it is so unfair! I cannot forget how genuinely clever and lovely I was when young: how joyfully ambitious, and with enough of an *entrée* at court to make things look possible. I didn't just marry an up-and-coming man, I married one I loved. I wanted to be a poet, a patroness of poets and philosophers; I wanted to be a great power behind a cosmopolitan court. I even thought, dear Gods, that it would be interesting to come to this strange country where the people are still in touch with an ancient and beautiful mythology, far richer and purer than ours. A real religion. And look at me now! I dupe my husband with nursery tales because he never listens to a word I say. I write vulgar letters full of cheap jokes because I have nothing else to do. I haven't written a decent line in years. I'm starved of reasonable company. I don't even read anymore, except the most trivial trash. Instead, I sit alone and fidget with my nail polish. I know perfectly well that we are stuck here where nothing, nothing ever happens, and we'll be here until I die of boredom or he makes such a major mess of things that we're sent somewhere even more boring. And then life will go on and no one will ever hear of me, or poor old Pontius Pilate, again. It does seem a pointless waste of all that practised charm, all that expensive perfume and all that energy that I put into the business of growing up.

You see, old friend, I have a bad case of the blues. So have some pity on me; send me some hot gossip, and even something decent to read. Give my love to anyone who might still want it, and if you have a chance, put in a good word for us at court. Pontius might at least amuse the Emperor with his mystical researches into pagan rituals.

Please, *please,* write soon, with love from your old school chum,

Claudia Procula,
Wife to Pontius Pilate, Supreme Governor of the Province of Palestine, under the august authority of our great Emperor, Tiberius Caesar

Why I Became a Plumber

'One of the problems for the menopausal woman, both
medically and socially, is the relative silence on flushing and
similar symptoms.'
  − *Pamphlet on the Menopause* (Boots the Chemist)

'One of the advantages of the double-trap siphonic system,
worth considering in some locations, is its relative silence on
flushing.'
  − *Simple Plumbing* (Cassells, 1989)

'One of the easiest ways to distinguish the Jack Snipe from
the Common Snipe is its relative silence on flushing.'
  − *Pocket Guide to British Birds* (Collins, 1966)

FOR MY SILVER WEDDING ANNIVERSARY my husband gave me a
garden; a garden of rich loam, south facing, well planted in
some distant past so that there were mature shrubs and fruit
trees and a white mulberry in the centre; but a garden which
had been more recently neglected so that there was lots of
work to do and decisions to make. And, because gardens tend
to come that way, this garden had a house attached to it - a
dear little house built of mellow brick which, on sunny days,
seemed to absorb heat and radiance through the day and then,
in the evening, give it off again so that the house glowed
warm after the sun had set.

I was delighted. It was the best present anyone could be

given. I thought my husband had bought it as a retirement home. In a sense this was true. What I had failed to grasp was that it was *my* retirement home, not ours. That after 25 years on the job of wife, I had been rendered redundant. The garden, and the house with it, was not a silver wedding present, but a golden handshake. The firm had engaged a new, bright young thing, who would do all my work and then some. I think I might have been able to bear it better if she had been some bimbo. I could then think of my husband as a naughty child, greedily meeting his desires as a child does. She was not. She was actually quite like me, but fifteen years younger. She loved him, and was sorry that all this had to happen to me. Quite likely it was she who insisted on my handsome pay-off.

I'm fairly certain though that it was not she who insisted on the way he chose to tell me. The first night in the new house we had sex and he made love with an exuberant energy – a renewal of a somewhat neglected interest – and then while my ribs still felt the weight of his presence, he informed me that this was the last time. I honestly think that he thought that if he gave me a really good rogering it would last me a nice long time and he would not have to feel guilty. Men, as no doubt you have noticed, are rather inclined to overestimate their own sexual performance. Given they are honest – though misled – about this, would you say that it was a kindly and generous impulse on his part, or a final arrogant cruelty? I had been sacked – sacked and looted and pillaged; perhaps it was only proper that I should be raped as well.

Then he pushed off – no doubt feeling that he had scraped through the whole embarrassing thing rather smoothly and that I had always wanted a garden, so everyone was happy. But I was not happy. I was in shock. For about ten weeks I just huddled in a heap.

Then I had a miscarriage.

Although it was nearly eighteen months since my last

period and I had given the matter no thought, I know a miscarriage when I have one – in fact, I'm a bit of an expert. I curled up in bed shaken by pain and waiting for the whole horrible thing to be over. Then I phoned for an ambulance and had them take me to the hospital for the tedious and nasty business of getting my poor weary womb scraped clean.

'Why don't we just take it all out for you?' they asked.

'No, thank you,' I said.

'Hormone replacement therapy is jolly good now, you know.'

'No, thank you,' I said.

I didn't tell my husband; I really felt that I could do without his guilt-driven sympathy just then.

They sent me home quite soon.

It was a few weeks after this that I began to hear the singing.

At first it was just odd notes, clear but off-hand, if you know what I mean. The sort of singing that you might get if a choirboy of considerable ability just happened to be singing to himself as he walked up the road outside my house.

The singing became more frequent and clearer and louder. There was nothing exactly scary about this because it was heart-wringingly beautiful music. On the other hand, if you are a woman of that certain age, who is just recovering from a distinctly female complaint and trying to get used to being dumped by her husband, even the most lovely music, welling up from an unknown source and filling your house with a joy you cannot share, is a bit disturbing. More disturbing, however, was the discovery – or rather the realisation – that the singing came from the loo. Peripatetic choirboys along rural byways are unexpected, but invisible choirboys in the downstairs lavatory are rather more than that.

Anyway, the singing, it transpired, did not come from the lavatory in general; it came quite specifically from the toilet bowl itself. It always stopped abruptly if I went in, but there would be a slight disturbance of the water – a quivering of ripples bouncing as though I had dropped a small stone into the pan. The music came up as solidly as the stone would go down.

I thought that perhaps my dead baby was crying for me. There was within the pure and lovely sound an unbearable sadness, a yearning, that called to me for love. The baby, I believed, wanted me as much as I wanted it. I tried to catch the singer out. I'd leap into the room the moment the music started, pouncing on the bowl. I'd leave the door ajar and try and sneak in on bended tiptoe. I even arranged a small net, hanging from the seat. Such techniques produced nothing, but I had to find out: quite apart from anything else, I was getting constipated as well as curious.

The long-wanted garden went undug. The kind letters from old friends asking me to spend the weekend with them, or inviting themselves to inspect my new home, went unanswered. I unplugged the phone so as not to disrupt my vigils in the hallway. I was consumed with longing and with concentration. I do not think I have worked so hard on anything since the day I finally realised and accepted that soufflé was, and forever would be, beyond my culinary capabilities.

Finally I tried something different. I went into the lavatory when it was silent. I crouched down beside the loo itself, but craftily – so that my head was not in the line of vision from anywhere near the water level. I waited. I waited through stiffness and discomfort, beyond cramp, long past boredom and way after sleepiness. And in the late afternoon, when a long yellow finger of sun angled itself through the window and, picking up every dancing dust mote on its way, just touched the surface of the water, I was rewarded. There was a gurgly noise, some frolicsome splashing, a gentle laugh, and then the singing started.

Quick as a thought I attacked. Swooping like a gannet on

its prey, I plunged both hands down into the water, grabbing wildly but efficiently at what I knew had to be there. I felt a thrashing, a fighting, then a despairing wriggle and finally a sudden relaxation, a dead weight against my palms. Alarmed, I drew them up and looked at what I had caught. Between the clenched fourth and fifth fingers of my left hand the end of a tail, moss green and scaled with silver edges, hung out. Where my thumbs and index fingers met there were strands of equally green, green thread. Without relaxing my attention for an instant, I struggled to my feet and took my trophy to the wash basin, and there inspected my catch. In my hands I held a very small mermaid.

She had fainted dead away, her tiny eyelids, grey-shadowed, covered her eyes and her long green lashes lay against her milk-white cheeks. I was not sure what you did with a passed-out mermaid. I could not push her head between her knees, because of course she had no knees. I placed her, looking decidedly seedy, into my primrose yellow pedestal sink. I felt worried and guilty. I reached for the cold tap and allowed a few drips to fall on her. Under her tiny but wonderfully full breasts I could see her ribs flutter to the beat of her heart; so I knew she was not dead. I picked up my cologne and waved the bottle under her nose – or, more accurately given the scale of things, over her face.

Suddenly she sneezed, sat up abruptly and said, 'Oh, a midday curse on the double-trap siphonic lavatory suite.'

Retrospectively I do not know what I thought a mermaid would say if she happened to recover from a shocking faint to find herself not only in a stupid pastel-coloured sink, but with an enormous, concerned face looming over her. Certainly not that.

I was startled into saying, 'What?'

'A double-trap siphonic toilet arrangement. That's what you've got and that's what's to blame for all this.'

Then suddenly she grinned like a child, and said, 'Excuse

me, that was rude; please remember I've never seen this end of you before, only the other end.' And when I gaped at her dimly, she giggled and added, 'It's a very nice bum actually; don't worry about it.'

She had brilliant green eyes, and this strange green hair and the tail and a stunning figure — which is quite a lot for someone so small to have all at once.

'Does it hurt if I touch you?' I asked.

'No,' she replied, 'it was the shock, not the pain that made me pass out.' So very gently, using only one finger, I stroked her head.

'That's nice,' she murmured. 'Could you put some more water in this pond, please?'

I turned the cold tap on and let it run until the sink was half full. She cavorted with pleasure, dancing and diving in the little waves. I thought, 'I'm going crazy.' Then I thought, 'So what? This is fun.'

When she felt comfortable she sat up, sort of bobbling on the water, and we looked at each other with open curiosity.

'Why did you grab me like that?' she asked, perhaps a little aggrieved.

'I just wanted to know what was going on; who was making the music,' I told her. Then I remembered that I had hoped it was my baby and, quite without my meaning to, I started to weep; not the wild angry tears of the weeks after he had left me, but sad sweet tears for the child I had lost and the body that had betrayed me. My tears splashed into the sink and the mermaid caught and drank them.

'Salt!' she cried, 'oh, sweet salt! And I thought I would never taste it again.'

This made me think, so I snuffled and sniffed a bit and asked, 'But why are you here? What are you doing in my loo?'

'I got stuck,' she said, almost shamefaced. 'It's all the fault of this newfangled plumbing.'

Involuntarily I glanced at my loo: it was one of those low-slung modern numbers. I had given its technology no thought. Until that moment I had never, I am ashamed to say, given any loo much thought; unless it were blocked and then my husband, in a manly way, had rung the plumber, who had usually complained that I had been putting unsuitable objects down it, and he and my husband would exchange that 'poor dears' look. Even thinking about this brought on a hot flush. I stood there while blood pumped up from below my waist and sweat pumped down my back and I felt a sulky expression, half shame-filled, half defiant, take over my features and I wanted to cry some more.

'What a pretty colour!' exclaimed my little mermaid, 'I'm very fond of pinks, they're so opposite from greens.' I felt better immediately and returned to the business.

'So, what's wrong with my loo?'

'It's one of those double-trap siphonic contraptions,' said the mermaid grumpily, 'I told you that already.'

'But I don't know what that means.'

'Well, you shouldn't have installed one then. From your point of view it means it takes up more space than the old-style works, but that is compensated for by its relative silence on flushing. And, of course, it uses less water which is important ecologically, but extremely unfortunate for me. From my point of view it means that I can't get back out into the mains water system – just like a salmon parr when someone builds a dam.'

(I never did discover what she had been doing in the freshwater channels in the first place – she could be a little shy about personal matters, and I've always hated being cross-questioned myself).

'Would you like something to eat?' I asked her – I could not imagine there was much nutrition in the sewage system.

'Thank you, but I don't eat,' she said politely, 'but could I have a comb and mirror, please? We are nourished by our own loveliness.' I noticed that as she said this her cheeks were suffused with the palest apple-green tinge – the mermaid equivalent of a blush, as I was to learn. It did make a lovely contrast with menopausal flush pink.

The mirror was easy, but a comb her size was hard. In the end I went into town and bought a Fashion-Barbie-Accessory-Selection.

'For your granddaughter, madam?' asked the smiling salesgirl.

'No, for my mermaid,' I said without thinking.

She gave me a distinctly fishy look. The day before I would have been embarrassed, but now I just giggled. This seemed to perturb her somewhat.

So, suddenly it was springtime; a greener spring than I had ever known and sparkling with promise and delight. Fresh gold greens of dawn; soft sweet greens of noontide; luminous thick greens of evening; and rich dark greens of dreams. And none of them as green, as fresh, as sweet, as rich, as varied as the greens of her tail and her eyes. None as green as her laughter.

I bought her a fish bowl, since I could not spend all my time in the hall toilet. The round one we tried first proved most unsatisfactory; it distorted our views of each other. So I bought the larger rectangular kind, and then realised that it was exactly the same as the crib in the Intensive Care Unit where my long-ago baby had died, and I cried.

To comfort me she sang – and to her singing I wept all the tears of the long years away, and was genuinely happy to see my husband when he called by about the divorce settlement. This seemed to perturb him somewhat.

She and I talked – and talking to her I became open and fluent and quick as a green highland burn. I rang my old friends and chatted, buoyantly, wittily, happily. This seemed to perturb them somewhat.

And, being knowledgeable in such matters, she taught me plumbing.

By the end of June, I was explaining politely to the man from the Water Board that I did know the difference between pressure and flow, so he did not need to patronise me. This seemed to perturb him somewhat.

In the middle of July I installed my own power-shower. (Bliss.)

And by August I had come to recognise how many women get and stay married because they are afraid of the plumber. I decided that that winter I would go on a car maintenance course and then I would not be afraid of anybody.

My mermaid checked that cars did not have dangerous slicing propellers and, once reassured, laughed and sang a high G so pure and glorious that the wine glasses reverberated, humming different notes in a perfect harmonic scale. To reward her for this stunt I took my engagement ring and had one of its emeralds taken out and made into a choker for her.

'What's it *for*?' asked the young jeweller, curious about mounting a single emerald (a very small one, we had been poor though optimistic then) on a fine gold chain less than two inches long.

'It's a necklace for my mermaid,' I said.

This seemed not to perturb him at all. He just smiled. When I went to collect the choker he had added two seed pearls, one either side of the emerald, and he did not charge for them. I laughed with pure joy. I might well be mad, but I was not alone in my madness and anyway, it was fun.

I was so happy that summer.

It took me until September; until the horse chestnut trees were dark matt green, and their shiny nuts crashed from the branches and lay, cradled in silk, inside their split shells. It took me until the evenings were heavy green, until the green flash on the cock-pheasant's neck stood out in the cut cornfields. It took me until autumn to accept that the little mermaid was not as happy as I was.

At first I did not notice.

Then I tried not to notice.

Then I pretended not to notice.

One evening we had a thunderstorm; green flashes of lightning across the green evening sky. And afterwards the air was pure and soft and cool and she sang. She sang that night so sweetly that two dog foxes came to sit in the garden to hear her; and a moth dechrysalised eight months early and thought death a cheap price to pay for such music. There was, within that pure and lovely sound, an unbearable sadness, a yearning that called to me for love.

So I said, 'Do you want to go back to the sea?'

Deep within her green eyes was a flash of desire, come and gone like a moon-bow in the spray of a waterfall. I started to weep again as I had not wept since the spring.

'Not much,' she said, but her eau-de-Nil flush betrayed her.

I had her at my mercy. I wanted to be mean and greedy and selfish and cruel. I needed her. I had a right to what I needed. All I had to do was pretend to believe her.

'You're not a good liar,' I told her.

I picked up her intensive care container and carried it out to the car. There were still the remnants of thunder in the air, but the sky was clearing. The moon appeared all silver furbelowed from behind a silver cloud.

It was 48 miles to the nearest coast, and I could not even drive fast because of sloshing her about. A slow mile for each year of my slow life. Anyway, I was crying all the time, which made driving particularly tricky.

When we reached the shore it was so late that it was early again, the dark paling enough to make a grey skyline far, far out to sea. There was a whispering, a murmuring of waves. I parked the car in some rough grass, as near to the pebble beach as I could go. I sat there for a long time and she watched me, silent now. There was the first movement of birds stirring out towards the end of the bay – duck probably, and higher, invisible, the drift of gulls. One of them cried out and I moved at last. I opened the car door and stretched. The stretching made me sneeze, and the sound of the sneeze flushed out a Jack Snipe couched in a tussock almost at my feet. It was still too dark to see that snakeskin pattern on its back, but I knew it by the fierce draught of its wings and its zigzag, silent departure. I cried out in shock and delight, and then turned and lifted the transparent tank from the passenger seat.

She just stared at me. I carried her down to the water's edge. The tide was full so it was not far enough. I lifted her out and held her for a moment.

She stretched up to her neck and I did not immediately understand what she was doing: she was trying to take off her necklace.

'No, keep it,' I said.

'Every time you flush your double-trap siphonic toilet,' she told me, 'in its relative silence, you will hear me singing.' I saw her green tears welling.

She reached up a tiny finger and touched my face.

I lowered my hands into the almost still water. It was shockingly cold. I don't have to do this, I thought. She can't make me. I'm bigger than her.

There was a frantic, powerful wriggle against my fingers and she was gone.

The pre-dawn air was suddenly bitter chill. I shivered. I could not see for tears and for my shaking. I turned away, stumbling on the shingle, groping for the hankie I never manage to have when I need it. Something made me turn back. Out there, in the free water, beyond the beach, I could see her. She was dancing in, on, with, the waves, lit by a green phosphorescence which had risen from the depths to welcome her home. Her tail was splashing joyfully. She was singing; I could hear her; she was singing a completely new song of

145

freedom and joy. Within that pure and lovely sound there was no sadness, no yearning. She sang to me with love.

She looked towards the beach, saw me watching and threw up her pale arms – not drowning, but waving.

And that's why I became a plumber.

The Pardon List

'WHY WOULD I DO that?' she asked him.

'To be safe,' he wanted to answer. He wanted her to be safe. He knew she had frightened people with the wild gleefulness of her dancing and laughing when they ambushed the manorial clerks and burned the court rolls. He knew in his own dark and, he feared, cowardly heart that they might need to punish her, if not now then sometime. One day, because they had all stepped outside their known space and abused the king's officials, because they had rioted, they might need to punish someone. One day they might look for someone who was theirs to pay for their sins – a scapegoat. Someone like her, who was theirs but whom they did not love.

They did not love her.

It is hard to love someone whose very existence makes you feel guilty.

Of course she does not remember now. For five nights she had wailed in the cottage – the first night fearfully, the second night angrily, the third night desperately and the last two reduced to periods of plaintive mewling; she was fifteen months old and of course she does not remember. For five days, in the terror of the pestilence, in the horror of the deaths and confusions, no one had thought to go and see what might be happening in the small cottage beyond the village. On the morning of the sixth day, her mother's brother, nervy and cross, anxious and guilty, had walked up the hill, pushed through the doorway into the living space and seen the carnage. Her mother, her father, her two brothers and the baby were all dead: their fingers and feet blackened and the sickly sweet smell of putrefaction filling the air in the cramped room, making it poisonous, making it dangerous. And the child with her face turned to the wall was huddled in the corner barely able to turn her head for weakness, but alive and untouched by the pestilence.

He was not a wicked man, just a harried and guilt-ridden one. He scooped her up and carried her as quickly as he could out into the sunshine. He knew he should have remembered to come sooner. It was too easy to feel that, if she had died too, it would not have mattered that he had not gone sooner and he would not have had to endure his own guilt. His wife, pregnant and panicked, could not bear to have the child near her. They gave her a place by the fireside, fed her as they might have fed a dog, but no one held her, or consoled her or comforted her. And yet it did them no good; her uncle's wife took the pestilence, the buboes swelled in her groin, her fingers turned black and the child in her belly died with its mother. Her uncle blamed her, spared her no kindness and made her work too hard from too young. Before she was three years old she had heard him trying too often to hand her into the care of someone else. But no someone else wanted the task. She seemed tainted – both too lucky in living and too unlucky in her fate. No one hurt her or beat her or starved her. But it was cold charity.

Cold charity, but she survived more or less and grew; never sweet, never pretty, never charming and even just to see her walking down the street was to remember they had left her forgotten in the charnel house of hell for five whole days.

She grew up before us like a root out of dry land. She had no form or comeliness, no beauty that we should desire her. She was despised and rejected by us, a woman of sorrows and acquainted with grief, as one from whom people hide their faces.

To be fair to them all, it was a very hard time. Half the people, five in every ten inhabitants of the small rural community died within a few weeks, died fast, inexplicably and horribly. Five in ten — and the fields unweeded, the harvest not fully gathered, the weather unfavourable and the fear palpable, nasty, guilt-inducing. Their Lord, away in Scotland with the king's army, offered them no succour, still demanding full rents and later clamping down hard on anyone who wanted to take to the road and find a better service. His Reeve required full serf labour though there were not the villagers to provide it and their own fields needed every hand they could find.

But everyone in the village knew they had left her in that cottage for five days wailing for help and just to see her outside her hovel scattering seed for her hens, or to watch her walk across the fields spinning rhythmically as she walked, or doing her share of the field work... just seeing her reminded them all that they were proved mean-hearted and un-neighbourly. So it was hard to love her. She had to get by without.

Now, more 30 thirty years later, she stood leaning against the jamb of her door, her spindle in her hand but her head uncovered. She looked up at Sir Matthew with an oddly quizzical expression.

'Why would I do that?' she asked.

Sir Matthew was a priest. Just, he had little Latin and no preferment. He was slightly older than her and markedly less chaste, and through that restless spring and fierce summer he had stirred up communities of protest across Essex. He knew that Wycliffe's teaching was convenient to him, served his own small greeds and ambitions, but he also believed that the fact that it suited his interests did not make it untrue.

So he taught that the new poll tax was contrary to the traditions of the kingdom and the will of God. That taxing married couples as two separate individuals was contrary to the one flesh that God had ordained they should become. That the failures of the war in France demonstrated God's displeasure and proved that the tax was unjust – its endless repetition impoverished the people even while it profited the powerful. That, when the King's fancy tax collectors came knocking, failing to declare individuals or lying about one's true prosperity was justified, even graced. That the hard-earned pence of the poor was wasted in corruption and indulgence and mismanagement by the great. And that to refuse to pay such taxes was holiness in the eyes of Christ.

He declared that the clergy should abjure all wealth, hold no office of state and preach the scriptures to the people in English. That the monks in their gated luxury, their Latin singing and their cruel exercise of power over their own unfree labour force were an abomination. With John Wycliffe he believed that, 'Englishmen learn Christ's law best in English. Moses heard God's law in his own tongue; so did Christ's apostles.'

He opened the scriptures to her and to anyone else who would hear him. He taught her that God had no tolerance for serfdom:

'By the law of Christ, every man is bound to love his neighbour as himself; but every servant is a neighbour of every civil lord; therefore every civil lord must love any of his servants as himself; but by natural instinct, every lord abhors slavery; therefore, by the law of charity, he is bound not to impose slavery on any brother in Christ.'

Or sister. Her freedom was guaranteed by God. In her he found a willing student.

Somewhere in the heady months behind them, while the roses flowered in the hedgerows, she and he had become allies, companions, perhaps friends. Today he had come down several miles to see her and she knew it and was grateful. But now the bright full green of June was darkening, fading towards autumn and the hawthorn berries were showing their first streaks of blood-red ripeness.

'Why would I do that?' she asked him.

His eyes dropped and were caught by the spinning whorl that weighted her spindle, dancing in response to the twitch of her elbow that kept it on the move; he realised that she was never perfectly still. He watched the smooth balanced block of wood that span and span, because he found he could not look straight into her face, into the new bright boldness of her eyes. He did not know how to answer her.

The rhythm of her spindle did not waver.

'Look,' she said, 'I did not assault the tax official. I did not burn the court rolls. But you taught me it was right to do so. Was it right? Are you saying now it was not right?'

He could feel the heat of her rage. He shook his head.

'I did not go into the Tower and kill the Chancellor. I wish I had, but I did not.'

After a pause, she added, 'I did not kill any of the Flemish weavers.'

He looked at her now, almost nervously.

'So,' she went on, 'what do you want me to seek a pardon for?'

After another pause she added, 'They cancelled the promises the boy King gave us; they took away the freedoms he promised us, just like that. I hear they are executing people – just like we did – only more of them. Are they seeking pardons? Are they putting themselves on the pardon lists?'

The smooth balanced block of her spindle weight span and span, holding the line of thread taut; and suddenly it looked to him like a body on a gibbet – and then, as he watched, it jerked, jumped from the true spin; her yarn tangled, but she ignored it. She said, very quietly, but clearly, calmly,

'They killed Wat. They killed him during a parlay. That is a sin. Do they seek pardon?'

Abruptly she looked down, saw the knotted mess of her spinning, gathered it in, licked her fingers, spliced the frayed thread back onto the loose yarn bundle, let the spindle drop, rolled it against her thigh and started the rhythmic process again. He could taste his own jealousy in his mouth. They were all like this about Wat Tyler – not just the women, the men as well. There was something about him; people loved him, followed him, honoured him. He was, he had been, a big rough man, not smooth or polite... but something, Wat Tyler had something Sir Matthew did not have and, of a sudden, he minded.

Once her weight was once more dancing smoothly she asked, 'So, Sir Matthew, why would I want to put my name on a pardon list?'

There was something bold about her, some high-handed flourish in her stance, something that had not been there before. Briefly he wondered what she had got up to and with whom in that wild fortnight, after she had danced so gleefully – so wantonly, he now thought – round the fire in the Manor Courtyard and had disappeared into the night and, he learned later, journeyed to London in that strange mixed movement, part mob, part army, singing and marching and praying, sermon-ed over by braver priests than he; burning and looting and killing, opening the prisons, killing the law officers, but also obedient to Wat Tyler and ordered and fearsome. He was, unexpectedly, frightened of her as well as for her. He found he could not look straight into her face, into the new bright knowingness of her eyes. He fidgeted with the knotted cord at his waist, looking sideways across her small barren yard.

'They say...' he began, then lowered his voice, almost muttering, 'they say you were... were you, were you at... the sacking... the burning... the Savoy Palace?'

'Oh they do, do they? Whoever "they" may be.'

There was a clarion note, half laughter, half pride in her voice and she was mocking him. He looked up and she seemed alight with a fierce joy, a strange triumphant fire. He looked away again.

'No, Matthew, we did not sack or loot the Savoy Palace, we cleansed it as the Lord Jesus cleansed the Temple. We were zealots for truth and justice, not thieves and robbers.'

There was a silence, and still he fixed his eye on the ground and watched as though counting one by one each blade of grass at her feet.

'Sir Matthew,' she said, reinserting the title of respect, 'You go around and about, you have been all over the land, I am sure you have seen many things, but I haven't. I have just stayed here – I thought our own Lord was grand and rich – and I did not know anything. Look at me, Sir Matthew, look at me.' She waited until he looked up; she smiled a smile of great sweetness and went on: 'I did not know there were so many beautiful things in the whole world as there were in the Savoy Palace. I do not mean just the rich things – the silver and the gold and the parcel-gilt and the jewels. There was lots of that stuff and very nice too for those who have it. Cart loads of treasure, and – as the Book warns us – it makes them proud and mean, it gives them power and swagger. But it wasn't that. It was all the lovely things, the truly beautiful things.

'There were books with pictures in them, shining big letters and pictures of Our Lord, a little baby, and his blessed mother and angels with wings of gold and trumpets raised – and all in colours so bright, and so tiny and so lovely. But there were not just beautiful things for God; there were beautiful things for Lords and Ladies. I went into a bedchamber, a huge room with a painted ceiling and a great bed all carved and coloured and curtained with hangings and on it, just thrown on it were great billowing cushions of goose feather down – more geese than we have in the whole village – just to make beautiful cushions for some Lady's beautiful head. The bed had a covering that was the softest thing I have ever touched, woven out of softness, made from some thread I do not know, like spiders' webs. And an embroidery on the wall that was sewn with flowers, more real, more lovely than the flowers in the fields in May — with tiny, tiny golden stitches and colours and all sparkled with jewels, with pearls and... and... You know, Sir Matthew, I am counted a good enough needlewoman — not just a decent spinster, who turns good sturdy yarn — but for needleworking also, nice straight little stitches, tidy, firm, but I cannot sew like that, so skilful and lovely and... I do not even know the words... I did not know there was sewing like that in the whole world. I did not know there were all these beautiful things — I did not know it even in my dreams. And now I know.

'And I know too that I am more powerful than all those beautiful things.

'I found a cup, a beaker made of glass, like the window in the Abbey, a little larger perhaps than my hand and with deep coloured lights in it. The light went into it and came out in sparkled colours. It danced for me and I wanted it, I wanted it so much. It was the finest, the loveliest thing I have ever seen. I almost thought I would keep it, tuck it into my tunic and no one would know. But we were not there as thieves and robbers. We were there for justice and truth.

'So I threw it at the wall. And it smashed, it smashed into a thousand pieces and they lay on the floor and they sparkled like the stars. The floor was dark, there was light coming in the window and the shards of that beautiful precious glass were sparkling on the floor like Our Blessed Lady's Highway does every night in the heavens. I made the stars dance in glory. Nothing, nothing in my life has been beautiful... until those little fragments of glass all the colours of heaven danced on the floor of that lovely, lovely bed chamber.

'So then I was a little crazy and it was glorious. We smashed up that palace, we broke all the things, or we tossed them into the river — ripping and breaking and singing and laughing. We were laughing. Hot, powerful, strong. We threw all those things into the river. And then we burned it down – and those hot red flames and black smoke rising matched the heat in me. I tell you, Sir Matthew, I believe that after all those years of meekness and gentleness and goodness, the Lord Jesus must have enjoyed smashing up the tables of the money lenders in the Temple. I hope he had as much joy of it as we did when we burned the palace. We were the vengeance of God and it was fun.

'Do you know something? When we broke into the Savoy Palace we found this little gaggle of grand ladies, and they were trying to hide, but squeaking like mice, and weeping and moaning and carrying on. Pissing themselves like as not, from fear. And we, the women I mean, were flighting them a bit, not very kind, but light-hearted, ragging like children do. But the men... well you know what men are. You could see they knew these women were beautiful, and they were beautiful, but so silly. And I dare say no better than they ought to be. But the men were... they were kissing their hands, all respectful and proper, and offering them safe passage, offering to be their escort, assuring them of their safety. And at first I felt small and dirty and envious, greedy towards them; I felt that they deserved the good treatment they were getting. But afterwards, after we had destroyed the beautiful things and set the palace aflame, I saw some more ladies like that out on the street, looking all frightened and foolish and I thought differently. I thought, "Well, the only difference between them and me is that they are cleaner. They get to have a bath as often as they want one. That's all." We had this song that Wat and Sir John Ball taught us. It goes, "When Adam delved and Eve span who was then the gentleman?" And I knew then that those fancy ladies are nothing. Nothing more than I am. I have changed.

'So they took back the promises of freedom that the boy King gave us; they killed Wat in front of our very faces and we did not save him; we slunk back home like whipped curs and they will say nothing has changed, nothing has changed, nothing has changed. But they are wrong. They will always be wrong, because all over this realm of England there are serfs, cottagers, poor men, villeins, women even who know the power of their own anger and know how good it feels to use it. Who have changed in themselves. Who know that we did not loot or rob the Savoy Palace the way they rob us. Who know that the only difference between serf and Lord is that they get to have baths. And to own beautiful things. We frightened them and they did not frighten us. So do not try to frighten me now, Sir Matthew.'

He was shaken, shaken by her strength, her bell-like clarity. He did not know what to say. He wanted to warn her, tell her to be careful – to keep her head down and not shout out her crazy triumph. He did not dare. He did not dare to confront her high, hot courage.

She dropped her hand, stopped the steady whirl of her spindle weight, grasped the long straight stick and poked him in the shoulder with it, hard enough to hurt. A more impertinent gesture would be difficult to imagine. He looked straight at her, taken aback, shocked by her unexpected cheek. She laughed at him, loudly, boldly and entirely without respect.

And then, her laughter sinking down, she returned his stare, smiled with an unexpected kindliness and said, 'I thank you for your care of me. But having committed no offence I need no pardon. And anyway I have never had so much fun in my life. I'll not be putting my name on any pardon list. Not now, not ever.'

True North

Far north, inside the ice circle, in the land of the long night, lived two women. One was a young woman and one was an old woman. The old woman must have known how they came to be living there, on their own, so far away from other people, but she never said. The young woman did not know – she remembered no other view than the long lifting of the snow banks and the chopped ragged ice in the sea below their home.

Because there was no one else, they did not need names for each other and used none. Because they had no community, they did not need to name their relationship either, and they did not do so. They never used the words mother or daughter or friend or sister or aunt, niece, cousin, lover. They just lived there together. Because there was no one to see, they did not know that the young woman was very beautiful and that the old woman was not. They knew that the old woman was full of ancient knowledge and useful skills, was wise in the ways of weather and seals, and knew all the hundred words for snow. The young woman was strong and rough and could run all day, a slow steady lope across the snow, in pursuit of moose herds, and she could crawl and slither over ice after seals and polar bears. And in the evenings the old woman could tell stories about the Seal Queen, and the lemmings maddened by each other and the winter fever who rushed into the sea; and her gums could chew, her hands could carve and her fingers could sew and plait and skin and braid. The young woman could sing and dance and let down her beautiful long hair and comb the thick dark mess until it glowed and sparkled with strange lights. And so they lived happily for a long time.

When spring comes inside the ice circle it is not with long rains and sweet emerging greenness. Instead there is the strange sound of the deep ice crashing and gonging as it breaks up – howling at night as it shifts and moves at last. The skeins of geese overhead break the stillness of the air with the powerful rush of their homecoming; and the she-seals are fat with promise and contentment. The light begins to seep back into the air; hardly noticed at first, the blubber lamp pales and the distant ice floes take on specific shapes. Where the winter freeze humped and pressured the sea into strange designs there is a new flatness smoothing itself back into water, but slowly.

And one year, with the spring, came something new. One morning when the young woman left the warmth of the ice house she saw, far away across the whiteness a new shape she had never seen before and heard, borne on the motionless air, a new noise, a swish-swish. The shape was dark and tall and it was not silent. In fear, she watched a while and the shape came nearer. She turned back into the ice house and told the old woman. And the old woman wrapped a polar fur around herself and came out. The shape had come nearer; it had a strange rising and falling gait, not the smoothness of an animal but rhythmic, lilting like the tune from a song. The shape was coming towards them directly and with purpose and both women were afraid, though for very different reasons: the young woman was afraid because she did not know what the shape was. The old woman was afraid because she did. It was a man.

He was a young man, tall and handsome. He was an ice traveller. He had spent the winter far from his village, all alone, because of a courageous but foolish error of judgement which had taken him too far to get back before the snowstorms and the darkness had come. He had wintered far from his own people and was now on his way home. He was surprised to discover this ice house; he had not known that anyone could go away and live so far from the village. Now, swishing on his wide snow shoes, swinging each leg wide of the other, his pack on his back, he came across the snow plateau and, seeing the smoke, thought of singing and company and warm meals cooked by someone not himself and a few days rest before he went on with his endless ice traveling.

The two women stood at the door of their home. With the necessary courtesy of people who live in such cruel terrain, it never occurred to them that they would not welcome him and feed him with whatever they had available and keep him in comfort until he was ready to travel again. In the pale light of the mid-morning he came towards them, slowly, swinging and swishing, and they stood there and waited for him. And when he came up they took him by the arms and led him into their home, and all three of them stood unwinding from their fur clothes in the light of the blubber oil lamp. And as she took off her seal skin jacket and pulled back her fur-trimmed hood, the young woman learned at last that she was beautiful, because his eyes told her so. And as she sank to her haunches to tend the cooking, the old woman knew that she was old and ugly, because his eyes did not even turn from the young woman.

Of course the young man loved the young woman; and the young woman loved the young man. Nothing else was possible with the spring crashing into life around them and both of them strangers to the other, and the young woman had never seen a man before and the young man was far from home on a courageous but foolish journey. Yes, they loved each other and the young man took the young woman to wife there in the ice house, on the fullness of the spring tides in front of the old woman and she said not a word, but squatted lower over the cooking pot and faded as the summer came. She could not hate the young woman, because she had known and lived with her for far too long and she could not hate the young man because she could see the rightness of this mating. But her sleep was disturbed by their loving and then by the dreams that came to her afterwards.

In some ways it was good to have the young man with them. With two hunters, both active and tireless and whose bodies know the curves and thoughts of each other's, there is hunting possible which cannot be done alone, and the piles of fur beside the house mounted and the young man talked of trading and possessions that the women knew nothing about – of drink that turned your head to fire and allowed you to meet the ancestors again and fight with the monsters; of fishing hooks and needles so fine and strong that they seemed magical; of colours and ribbons and beads and clothes that the women thought were parts of stories and not real though he told them over and over again. He took the old woman's skins in his hands and admired them and said that she had more skill with the knife than anyone, man or woman, he had ever seen and the skins that she handled would fetch higher prices. And he picked up the carvings she did, in bone and rock, marvelling how the walrus and the bear and the fish were revealed growing there. These too they could trade and he described the things that he and the young woman could have if they sold the carvings the old woman had made. And she who had carved for delight alone, through the long winter, wanted to snatch back her animals from his hands and hide them, but she did not. She did not because the muscles on his neck stood out like the sinews of the moose, and his legs were sturdy, strong and planted firmly in the ground, and his hands were driving into her heart and gut with their strength and beauty, and because the white horn of his nails made her think of the new moon. But she did not trust him.

And she was right. One day the young woman came to her and said that they were going away. She did not think about the old woman left alone in the ice house when winter came again; she did not think about the cold wind and the wildness to be endured alone. She said that he had made a sledge for her, each runner a rib of a great he-walrus that the young man had killed for her; he had worked on the sledge secretly when the old woman thought that he was hunting or walking or fishing. She said the sledge was the most beautiful thing she had ever seen; each runner was intricately carved; the seat was lined with pale fur; the seal sinews were so strong and taut that she would ride without a jolt across the frozen wastes. He would take her to his village and buy for her beads and jewels and garments worthy of her beauty. The young woman told the old woman that her husband was going to take her away from this dreary desolation, and this empty lonely life, and bring her to a place where her beauty would be appreciated and reflect credit on him. She told the old woman also that there was a child growing in her, that she hoped for a son as lithe and fine and strong as the young man, that she would have a son and a place where her beauty could be admired.

She desired the beauty of the young woman; she desired the child of the young woman; she also desired the husband of the young woman; and she had little enough to do all day except feed those desires. So they ate into her, like the ice of the approaching autumn, creeping up the rivers of her blood. Soon the couple must be gone, because the courage and foolishness of the young man were diminished by the loveliness of his wife and his tenderness for her, and he wanted to be in his village safe and certain before the hard weather and the long night came. The time was approaching when the old woman could wait no longer. One day the young man was gone from the house, so the old woman said to the young woman that it was a long, long time since she had braided up that beautiful hair. She said that they should prepare a special feast for the young man and that the young woman must look her most beautiful. The young woman was pleased; she felt that the old woman had not entered into her joy and had withdrawn from her recently so she was happy to find that she had been mistaken. So she unpinned her long hair and sat cross-legged on the floor at the feet of the old woman. The old woman took the comb made from bone which she had carved many years ago for the young woman and began to comb her hair. And she combed and combed. She revelled for the last time in that living loveliness; the hair shone and shook in the light of the lamp and sparkled like the sea-deep does in midsummer when it is crazed by the lights of the underworld that float up and dance on the surface. The young woman told her to hurry, eager to see her beauty in the admiration of the young man. So then the old woman took the hair and began to twist and braid it into a fat rope, and she took the rope and wound it round the young woman's lovely cream-colored neck and pulled and pulled, tighter, until the young woman was dead. Then she took her little hand knife, which she had made herself for skinning, down from the wall and, using all her immense and practiced skill, she skinned the young woman's face, not spoiling the hair, which was both lovely and necessary, not pulling out one eyelash nor missing the soft curves of lip and cheek. And when the young woman was faceless and bloody she dragged her out of the house and buried her in the soft snow of a drift not far away. Then she took a broom and swept the house and the snow with great attention so that no blood and do drag lines and no mess could be seen. Then she took a soft seal skin shift that she had made herself for the young woman and put it on; its gentle folds caressed her skin and everything seemed possible for her. She washed in ice water, the coldness of it bracing her joyfully. After all that, she took the skin from the face of the young woman and, with delicate practice of the years, smoothed the young woman's face over her own. Its lovely pliability covered the wrinkles and jutting bones of her old, ugly face; she pulled the creamy skin of the neck down as far as it would go, securing it with an ivory pin to the top of the soft shift; she tugged the heavy mass of hair back over her own thinning greasy locks and shook her head so that it fell loose again, covering the seamlines. And then she lay on the bed that the young couple had made themselves, and covered herself with furs and skins under which they lay night after night, leaving her outside. The thought of what she had done warmed her; the thought of what was coming heated her. She lay there waiting, ready and eager.

The young man came home. She heard the gentle rhythm of his snowshoes; she heard him banging off the spare snow and stomping about outside the house; she heard his muffled breath as he pulled his skin-jacket over his head; she heard the soft whistle that he always made when he was tired but pleased with himself. He came in. And seeing her lying on the bed all beautiful and waiting for him, he smiled. Where was the old one, he asked. And she told him that she had gone to the beach to look for a special stone for carving, to be a present for them at their departure, a very special carving as a bride gift and a gift for the child. The young man said that that was good because such a carving by the old hag would fetch a good price from some white-skinned collector and he laughed. The old woman would be gone for hours on such a task. The young man tugged at his boots; then he pulled off his shift, his trousers. His chest was muscled and beautiful, his loins were leaping for his bride, he fell upon her and she, kicking back the blankets, received him in her eagerness. He plunged into her body and she responded with delight. He was so far into his joy and lust that he did not notice the changed body. He plunged and bucked like the melting of a river when the great chunks of ice are hurled suddenly into the sea; he melted into her like the full tide of spring; and she leaped up for him like a young seal taking to the water for the first time. He rode her like the porpoise schools, she held him like the ocean deep.

There was a love and a knowing in them both.

He worked her like an old bull walrus and it was hot hard work and at last he was done and lifted his head and smiled down into her eyes. And the sweat from his joyful labour dripped from his forehead down the fringe of his black hair and fell onto her face. It shrivelled the skin, because the old woman had not had time for proper curing. The skin of the young woman shrank and curled away from the face of the old woman. Where it was secured at the neck with the ivory pin it tore away; from around her mouth the lips peeled back revealing her thin tired gums. The bones of her cheeks broke through the tenderness of the young woman's skin. The tears that sprang in her eyes rolled away the young woman's soft velvet and uncovered the harsh wrinkles. The hairline parted under the strain - the thick hair falling backwards onto the pile of bed-skins, the forehead dissolving, shrinking and disappearing.

With his hands he completed the work his sweat had begun, scrabbling at her face, scratching her, making her bleed. She herself did not move. Still naked, still lying on her, his lower body still replete with joy, the horror came into his eyes. The young man screamed and leapt to his feet; he grabbed for his shift, his breeches and boots and rushed out into the gathering gloom. She heard him retching and gasping as he fumbled the straps of his snowshoes. She heard his heaves and moans as he gathered what was necessary from around him. At last, she heard the swishing, swishing mixed with his horror, repulsion and guilt. The noises died away into the twilight, diminishing, fading and finally, after many, many minutes, finally gone.

And then the old woman was alone.

A Note On This Selection

THE STORIES IN THIS edition were individually selected by friends, colleagues and family members.

'Moss Witch' was chosen by David Borthwick.

'A Fall from Grace' was chosen by Harriett Gilbert.

'Andromeda' was chosen by Michelene Wandor.

'The Beautiful Equation' was chosen by Will Anderson and Ford Higgson.

'Miss Manning's Angelic Moment' was chosen by Peter Daly.

'Hansel and Gretel' was chosen by Mildred, Mark and Zoe Watson.

'The Edwardian Tableau' was chosen by Iona Lawrence.

'Rapunzel Revisited' was chosen by Adam Lee.

'The Swans' was chosen by Janet Batsleer.

'The Eighth Planet' was chosen by Matt Hoffman.

'Claudia Procula Writes a Letter' was chosen by Ruth Mathews.

'Why I Became a Plumber' was chosen by Jo Garcia.

'Seeing Double' was chosen by Mandy Merck.

'Her Bonxie Boy' was chosen by Ruthie Petrie.

'The Pardon List' was chosen by Ra Page.

'True North' was chosen by Richard Coles.